Scarlet

SUZANNE DE NIMES

NEON

A NEON PAPERBACK

This paperback edition published in 2006 by Neon
The Orion Publishing Group Ltd.
Orion House, 5 Upper Saint Martin's Lane
London WC2H 9EA

A CIP catalogue record for this book is available
from the British Library.

Printed and bound in Great Britain by
Mackays of Chatham.

ISBN 1-905619-08-5

ONE

Samantha gazed up at Jeremy's bronzed features, and his steel blue eyes stared down into the radiance of the girl's own sapphire irises.

Jeremy's strong jaw was clenched tight; he tried to betray not the slightest hint of emotion. But he failed and glanced away for a moment, towards the iridescent blaze where the setting sun was sinking into the tropical waves of the turquoise ocean. She could not help but admire him, his lithe and muscular body clad within a stylishly tailored safari suit.

"Samantha," he whispered, and his lips trembled as he uttered the three syllables of her name.

The girl reached out and took his left hand in her right. His grip was warm and firm. She noticed his pulse. It was racing as fast as her own pounding heart.

The man looked at her once again, and she smiled, her perfect teeth gleaming white against her Caribbean tan.

"Samantha," he repeated.

"Yes?" she prompted.

"I've . . . I've been a . . . a fool, such a fool," he admitted, hesitantly.

"So have I," she breathed.

"No, no!" he denied, rapidly, and he took her right hand in his left, enfolding her delicate fingers in his broad palm.

Simultaneously, they stepped closer towards each other until they were almost touching.

"Can you ever forgive me, Samantha?" Jeremy requested, urgently. "Will you ever forgive me, Samantha?"

3

Their eyes were locked together, and Samantha felt herself becoming lost in the infinity of the tall man's dominant gaze.

"Please," begged Jeremy.

Samantha's long blonde hair cascaded across her shoulders as she shook her head. She shook her head not in denial, however, but in confusion and bewilderment. Did Jeremy sincerely believe that she would not forgive him? One kiss was all she needed, one kiss and all of her darling's transgressions would be forgotten as well as forgiven – forever.

Samantha tilted her delicate face upwards; Jeremy bent his sculptured head downwards. The girl parted her mouth slightly, and a moment later her soft lips met the man's eager mouth.

They kissed.

They kissed with total ardour and with absolute devotion, with complete passion and with ultimate affection.

And with that one kiss they pledged the rest of eternity to one another.

This was not the end, it was only the beginning."

I stretched, yawned, picked up my mug of coffee, realised it was empty, put it down again, then stood up and walked over to the window. At one time my desk was against the window, but the view of the shops opposite and the flats above them had never been very inspiring. Now I preferred to face a blank wall, where the only things to look at were the cracks in the plaster. That tended to make me concentrate on the blank screen of my computer – and make sure it didn't remain blank for very long.

The two workmen on the scaffolding on the block opposite were still there. I had never seen them do any work; they seemed to spend most of their time watching the people go by below them, waving and whistling at the girls from the shops and offices. But I suppose if anyone ever watched what I did, it wouldn't seem that I ever did any work. It might appear that all I did was drink coffee, gaze at the wall, or at the ceiling, or play with my paperclips. Or maybe I would read the newspaper all morning, then watch some television. But that was work – it was called "research".

The men both saw me, and they immediately waved and shouted at me. This had been going on all week and I had made absolutely no response. But their reaction was instinctive; as soon as they saw a girl, any girl, they obeyed their male programming.

They were both wearing protective helmets and heavy boots, which looked out of place with their cut-off jeans. After a few seconds, they looked away. One of them inspected the masonry behind him, as if he were about to start work. Then the other opened a pack of cigarettes, offering one to his mate, who turned around again. They both watched the world go by as they smoked, hooting and yelling as a girl in short skirt passed beneath them.

The girl was wearing more than I was. All I had on was a loose T-shirt and a pair of cotton panties. It was too hot and humid for anything more. I had the window wide open in the hope of some relief from the sweltering city heat. All I got, however, was traffic noise and fumes.

This wasn't the way I'd thought it would all turn out. I'd always wanted to be a writer, and in that I had succeeded. But I wasn't writing what I originally thought I would. I had planned to write serious novels, great works of art which would be critically acclaimed and win literary awards. I'd begun to write the novels. The only trouble was: nobody wanted to publish them; nobody recognised them for the great masterpieces that they were. And, by now, even I knew they were not particularly good.

So I made a living writing for the women's magazine. It was a precarious living, but I didn't need much to get by – and maybe, someday, I really would write a book was worth publishing. Until then, I had to turn out formula stories about people with names like Samantha and Jeremy. I also wrote the occasional article or did interviews with various "celebrities". I'd tried my hand at every type of freelance journalism, but I preferred writing fiction. It was no good me trying to write about cooking, because the limit of my culinary expertise was beans on toast. It would be similarly pointless attempting anything on knitting or sewing or crocheting or embroidery. I didn't know the difference between a princess and a duchess, which eliminated the possibility of doing features on royalty. That didn't leave much else to write about . . . except Samantha and Jeremy.

Whenever I gave characters ordinary names like Debbie and Wayne, or Sharon and Gary, the editors always changed them to something like Alexandra and Tyrone. But I don't suppose there are many millionaires named Wayne or Gary, and it was always best to have a wealthy male protagonist. The men had to be tall and dark, rich and mysterious. The girls had to be beautiful and innocent. They would meet, she would fall in love with him, then believe she'd been betrayed – there was usually "another woman" involved, older and manipulative – but then at last it would turn out happily. Everything was best set against an exotic background.

It was all fantasy, harmless romantic escapism. And right at that moment I could have done with some escapism myself. A Caribbean island would have been ideal, which was perhaps why I'd written about one, although any beach would have done. A millionaire would have been similarly ideal.

In fact anyone might have been ideal. It wasn't only escapism that I needed: it was romance.

I stepped back into the room, out of sight, but kept looking at the two guys on the scaffolding. Although their bodies were hard and tanned, just like Jeremy, their arms were tattooed, their faces unshaven. That would never have done in a story, although it didn't bother me. I preferred the denim shorts to a safari suit, although I would have preferred them without the shorts. I tried to imagine the two men wearing just their helmets and boots, the way girls in men's magazines wore nothing but high heels, and I smiled at the image.

But I continued watching the two men, and I let my mind wander. I'd noticed them climbing down the scaffolding two days ago, how they'd gone into the pub on the far corner after work. They probably did that every day, which meant they would be there this evening. I could wrap a skirt around my waist, put on my sandals, and happen to meet them there. They would offer to buy me a drink, and I would refuse, saying that I was waiting for someone. Then I would relent, accept a drink from one of them, then a drink from the other. They would keep gazing at me, studying my body, and the more I drank the more I would welcome their attention.

And inevitably we would end up here, back in my flat. They knew why they were there, and I knew why they were there. Although there were two of them, only one of me, they were the ones who were unsure exactly what was to happen next.

I took the lead, kicking away my sandals, twisting out of my skirt, casting aside my T-shirt and thumbing down my

7

white briefs. I gazed at them, my legs astride, my hands on my hips.

"Who's first?" I asked. "What have you got to offer me?"

Their belt buckles were rapidly unfastened, their zips quickly undone, and their cut-offs came off. There was little to judge between the two of them, or between their rampant cocks.

"Okay," I said, smiling as I beckoned them towards them. "I can take you both on."

Which I proceeded to do – and they kept their helmets and boots on all the time.

I smiled again, thinking about helmets, then sighed. There was nothing wrong with a fantasy, even an erotic fantasy. I walked away from the window and headed for the kitchen. It was time for another drink. It seemed that I spent my whole life drinking coffee, that the more I drank the more pages I could write.

I noticed my nipples had become erect and were pushing through the thin fabric of my damp T-shirt. It was too hot to wear, and I peeled it off.

There was the last of a carton of orange juice in the fridge. I poured it into a glass, added some ice from the freezer, tasted it, then realised something was missing. Hunting through the back of the cupboard, I found the vodka bottle. There was an inch left at the bottom, and I added half to the glass of orange. I miscalculated, and there was only quarter of an inch left. That wasn't worth keeping, so I poured the rest of it out before making my way back and sitting down at the desk.

My nipples were still firm and very pink. I'd once been very daring and used the word "nipples" in one of my stories, but it had been edited out. Romantic heroines didn't have

nipples. It was perfectly acceptable for the magazine to publish an article about breast feeding, and even to use photo-
graphic illustrations, but it was utterly taboo to suggest that
breasts might serve another function; that it might not only
be babies who enjoyed licking and sucking at a ripe tit, and
that it might also be very pleasurable for the owner of the
boob to receive such attention.

If nipples were not permitted, then cunts were totally
forbidden. There must be a complete blank between the
heroine's "long legs" and "slender waist". I remembered
seeing some old black and white pictures of nude girls, and
their genitalia had been photographically erased. No pubic
hair, no *mons veneris*, no anything. As for fictional heroes,
who would ever know what was beneath their tight designer
trousers? The most we could get away with was "his manhood grew" or "his ardour was aroused" – and even then
nothing was ever done with it. The curtain fell, the screen
grew dark, or else . . .

I took a gulp of my drink and read through what I'd just
written.

"What a load of crap," I muttered, shaking my head.

This was not the end, it was only the beginning.

That was true, I realised. The story stopped just where it
was beginning to get interesting. My hero and heroine were
alone on a tropical beach at sunset, their arms around one
another, their tongues down each other's throat. That wasn't
the time to stop. I drank some more of my drink, stared at the
blank wall for a few seconds, then looked down at myself.
My body was damp with sweat, as though I were actually on
a Caribbean island. I had never been on one, of course, but
that's the job of a writer: to imagine, to make things up.

My idea of a tropical island came from old movies and from

television adverts for everything from rum through to chocolate bars. My idea of the perfect hero came from what I'd read, everything from *Wuthering Heights* to each issue of the magazines for which I wrote. My idea of a heroine came from . . . myself, I suppose.

I knew I wasn't as naïve and dumb as my heroines, no one could be, but I recognised that certain aspects of my personality inevitably came through in everything I wrote. Samantha was nothing like me physically. She was small, slim, delicate, blonde. I was taller, more curvy, with a wild mane of red hair.

The red was genuine – and a stray wisp curled out from the edge of my briefs, I noticed as I gazed down again. I took another drink, then looked back at the story. It was ready to be printed out and mailed to the editor. But it wasn't over.

My fingers hovered over the keyboard, and then I resumed typing.

'Their tongues clashed fiercely, pushing and probing against one another, advancing and then retreating, pausing while their teeth nibbled at each other's lips.

Samantha's firm breasts were pressed tight against Jeremy's chest, and she could feel the damp heat of his flesh through the flimsy fabric of her dress. Her nipples dilated as Jeremy forced his right leg between her thighs, pushing firmly upon her crotch, rubbing himself against her. After a few seconds she felt more pressure upon her hip and realised that it was his hardening prick. Samantha thrust herself ever nearer, enjoying the way she was stimulating him.

Jeremy's right hand slid down her back, over her tight buttocks and down to the edge of her short dress. He lifted the hem, his roving fingers making their way up her thigh and onto her silken panties. They inched their way up, over the

10

waistband, and then back, descending until his hand was upon the warm roundness of her bottom.

While this was happening, his left hand glided within the top of her dress, down through her bra and onto her bare breast. Her cupped her flesh in the palm of his hand, teasing the already hardened nipple with his thumb.'

That was more like it, I thought. I stroked my left breast with my right hand, while my left slid down over my left buttock. I studied what I'd written, making sure the logistics of the operation were correct, and I continued touching myself while I decided what was to happen next.

Despite the heat, Samantha was wearing a bra. Otherwise she was clad in a sundress and pair of satin panties. Jeremy was wearing his stupid safari suit. But whatever they both wore, it had to go. I raised my glass with my left hand, while the fingers of my right kept circling my nipple. It was nice just to touch myself, but there was work to be done. Another drink, and then I continued typing.

'Jeremy's hand began to withdraw from Samantha's breast, and she sighed in disappointment. But she need not have worried, because a moment later she felt his fingers on her back, undoing the buttons of her dress, finding the clasp of her bra and then expertly unhooking it. Her own hands had been exploring the man's taut body, and now she accepted Jeremy's lead and reached for his belt buckle.

The clasp soon came free; the button at the top of his pants proved no obstacle; and then she discovered the zip and tugged it down. His cock burst free of its confinement, thrusting up proudly above his underwear. She took his thick penis in her right hand, gauging its weight and length with her admiring fingers. She could feel the blood surging through his virile flesh, and his pulse was pounding faster than ever – and so was her own.'

So was mine, I had to admit, and I took another drink before continuing.

'Samantha's hand began to move up and down, manipulating Jeremy's warm prick, feeling it grow even more in her firm grasp. Her left hand pushed his pants down out of the way, and then she cupped his balls in her palm. At her touch, his scrotum tightened. The girl felt her dress and bra fall away as Jeremy pushed them down, and she shrugged free of them, releasing the man's gorgeous dick for a moment, then reclaiming her prize once her clothes had dropped to the sand.

All she wore was her panties. Then she gasped because it was Jeremy's turn to follow her direction, and his fingertips stroked across the soft silk of her briefs, over her pubis, then down between her legs and across the contours of her cunt.

His index finger found her cleft and eased itself within, pressing the silk into her inner labia. The fabric became instantly moist from the girl's inner juices. Samantha's twat lips began to swell at Jeremy's touch, and she moaned as he discovered her clitoris and began gently kneading it.'

I moaned, too – and discovered I was typing with one hand. My left hand was over my crotch, the index finger manipulating my swollen clit through the cotton of my damp knickers.

As I watched my fingers at work, in a way it was as if this had nothing to do with me. It was not my body, my hand, my cunt. It was simply something I was describing, making up. But I couldn't deny the waves of pleasure which were rippling up from my crotch.

I normally used my right hand when I masturbated, so

12

when I used my left it was almost like someone else was fingering me. I slipped my hand inside my briefs, touching my cunt directly for the first time. After a few seconds, I pushed my panties down out of the way, opened my legs wider. Meanwhile, my right hand kept on typing.

'The girl parted her thighs in encouragement, and Jeremy knew what she wanted, what she needed. His index finger worked expertly on her clitoris, while his thumb and middle finger rubbed against her labia. She trembled with delight. Each time he stroked her, she slid her hand up and down his shaft, wanking him, her encircled fingers moving from his hairy testicles up to the smoothness of his glistening glans, then down again.

He removed his hand, but it was only for an instant so he could glide his probing fingers into her panties. His other hand slid the silk down over her thighs, while his fingers slipped through the blonde nest of pubic hairs which veiled the heart of her femininity, making their way into her slick vagina, discovering and then deftly rolling her clitoris between his fingertips.

She gasped as he rapidly brought her towards the ultimate peak of sensation, then cried out triumphantly as she achieved an ecstatic climax.'

I had to stop typing then, losing coordination as I came. The inexorable tide of orgasm washed across me, draining me for several seconds. I was soaking wet, and not only with sweat.

"Wow!" I said, and that was not a word I used often.

I drew my left hand away from my hot cunt. I leaned back in the chair, reached for my drink and swallowed what was left in one thirsty gulp. There were a few pieces of ice in my mouth and I rolled them around on my tongue, then picked them out with my left hand, smelling my own feminine odour on my fingertips. I held the ice against my pubic hairs, allowing it to melt and trickle down into my labia.

Glancing at the computer screen, I began reading what I had just written.

'Their tongues clashed fiercely, pushing and probing against one another . . .'

Perhaps I had been trying to cool myself off with the ice, but as I read I began to heat up again. The ice melted more swiftly, but I rubbed what remained into my cunt. I knew I wasn't really trying to lower the temperature of my vulva, because the focus of my attention was my still erect clit.

I climaxed once more at the same time Samantha did, and this time all I could do was close my eyes and sigh with absolute pleasure.

Boy fucks girl was much more fun than what I was used to writing, although somewhat more exhausting – but it was the kind of exhaustion I liked.

And it was the only kind available to me . . .

What else is a girl expected to do? All I had were my fingers. They were my only company in bed. Or in the bath. Or in the shower. Right hand, left hand, fingertips, knuckles. Whatever lubricant was available, whether saliva or soap or baby oil. Or else there was always my multi-speed, variable-attachment, super-pulsating, all-thrusting vibrator.

Finally, I allowed my eyes to open. The screen was directly in front of me, its cursor blinking on and off at the end of the last line. Except that it wasn't the last line. Just as Samantha and Jeremy's story could not end when they kissed, neither could it stop here.

I needed another drink, but there was nothing else left in the fridge until I went shopping. I needed a shower, but that could wait. My needs, however, were nothing compared to poor Jeremy's.

The guy had given Samantha a magnificent climax, but he was still standing with his pants around his ankles, his cock thrusting optimistically up in the air. He deserved more than that, despite his safari suit. The least that Samantha could do was jerk him off, or maybe she could give him more . . .

With some effort, I devoted all my attention on the keyboard. This time I was using all my fingers as I typed:

'Samantha's hands had never stopped working on Jeremy's tool, even during the orgasmic pyrotechnics which had engulfed her entire being. Now she fell to her knees upon the sand, still grasping Jeremy's rampant phallus. Then she leaned forward in order to worship the idol before her, kissing the underside of the shaft before opening her mouth wide to engulf the dome of its engorged head.

Jeremy thrust his hips forward, and his cock flesh slid further between the girl's wide lips. She could taste his maleness, smell the pungent odour of his manhood, and there was no more powerful aphrodisiac. Samantha's tongue encircled the offering and her lips sucked eagerly, her fingers feeding the surging knob even deeper into her hungry mouth. The man gripped the back of her head, urging her to swallow him even more. His glans glided across the roof of her mouth, while her saliva ran down his cock. She stroked his balls with one hand, gripping what was left of his tool with the other.

The girl felt the potent shaft tremble, a volcano about to erupt, and she waited for the geyser to blow, the hot spunk to explode into her mouth and flow down her waiting throat.

Before this could happen, Jeremy suddenly pulled away. Almost without realising what was happening, Samantha found herself lying on her back upon the warm sand. Jeremy was above her for a moment, ripping off his jacket and shirt. Then they were both naked, his body came down upon hers, limb to limb. His prick was wet with her saliva, and it slid straight into her welcoming cunt.

They began to fuck.'

I stopped and stood up. That was enough. I couldn't take any more. Maybe I felt too jealous.

I went over to the window and leaned on the sill. The two workmen opposite almost fell off the scaffolding. I'd forgotten that I was nude, and so I backed away from the window and returned to the screen – and deleted all of the new section.

Then I switched on the printer and began to print out the original story. While that was happening, I took a long cool shower.

Dry, dressed in fresh panties and a clean T-shirt, I checked through the printout and made a few corrections and changes. But I kept remembering the part of the story that had existed for a few brief electronic minutes before being erased. It had been enjoyable to write, much more than enjoyable.

I had two calls to make, and I went over to the telephone and punched out the first number.

TWO

One of the phone calls had been to Don, and we arranged to meet for a drink at seven o'clock. That meant he would probably arrive at seven-thirty. So I arrived at eight o'clock, in case he'd guessed I knew he would be half an hour late, which meant he would be even later. He was only ever on time with his deadlines. In that he was totally reliable, or so he claimed.

It wasn't that I minded going into a bar on my own, not if I only had to wait five or ten minutes. But fending off every other guy in the place for any length of time became a drag.

Don was already there, a pile of books and papers on the table in front of him. It was evening by now but still very hot, yet he was wearing a jacket and collar and tie. He always wore a shirt and tie, although it was only a matter of luck if they happened to match his jacket. If they did, he would ruin it by wearing trousers that were five years out of style or a pair of shoes that were completely the wrong colour. His glass was almost full, which for most people would mean they hadn't been there for long; with Don it was hard to tell. He glanced up as I entered, then carried on reading. Ever the gentleman, he allowed me to buy my own drink.

I ordered a bottle of beer. Don wouldn't need another drink for a long while. I could out-drink him any time, and I frequently had done.

"How's it going?" he asked.

"Fine," I said. "You?"

"Wonderful, completely wonderful!"

Nothing was ever ordinary with Don, everything was always totally terrific – even when it was absolutely awful.

"I finished a story today," I told him.

"Fantastic!" He raised his drink in a toast. "To your latest miniature masterpiece." Our glasses clinked together.

"Masterpiece . . . ?" I said.

"If it's by you, how could it be otherwise?"

"True," I agreed, and we both laughed, then drank. "What have you been up to?" I asked.

"Did lunch with the executive producer today," he said, "and she just loves the treatment. She's got a meeting with the Europeans next week. Then next month she'll be in Hollywood, tying up things there. Once the cable and satellite and video deals are confirmed, we'll be ready to roll!"

"Great," I said, trying to be as enthusiastic as Don was.

Throughout the time I'd known him, Don had been writing screenplays. I'd lost count of the number of times he said he was about to sign a movie contract. He believed it, and he made everyone else believe it too, but it never happened. The nearest he had ever come to movie writing was reviewing films for one of the magazines for which he wrote.

He was in a similar position to me, both of us frustrated in our original ambitions. But at least Don was still trying to write a movie, and he was far more likely to succeed than I was. I'd never sell a novel if I didn't write one. Meanwhile, we both survived on magazine work. Whereas my material was aimed at a female audience, I knew that his stuff was definitely aimed at a male readership.

Neither of us, of course, had ever read any of the commercial work that the other had written.

We'd met at a writers' workshop two years previously, a weekend where authors got together to read and criticise each other's work. It was the first time either of us had been there, and also the last. The place was full of would-be poets, who read out terrible and interminable verses. It was so bad that even Don was driven to drink. We escaped to a nearby pub, which was also the first and last time I ever saw him get drunk.

He was so drunk I had to take him back to our hotel, he'd never have found it on his own. Even then, he couldn't find his room. The easiest course was to take him to mine, where he collapsed on the bed almost immediately. It was a large bed, and I was tempted to leave him lying there and climb in the other side. The weekend hadn't been much fun, up until the last few hours with Don, and so I decided to have some more amusement with him. It wasn't often that I had a helpless man in my clutches.

I undressed him, which wasn't very difficult. His glasses were the first thing to go, and I worked my way down. Although he was a few years older than me, Don has always had a kind of child-like innocence about him. Even his dick seemed child-like, so small and helpless. If I'd been more sober, I would never have done it what I did next; if I'd been less sober, I couldn't have.

Very lightly, I stroked his limp cock. It responded immediately. The flesh had a life of its own, beginning to uncurl and pay attention to what was happening. I watched in fascination as Don's tool became erect at my touch, growing thicker and longer, its domed head freeing itself from the foreskin, its single eye gazing hopefully around in search of a warm and damp aperture into which it could slide.

That night was a real revelation, because I had final confirmation that a man and his penis are two separate things.

19

It's the cock which is always awake, always in command. And if you can control a guy's tool, you can control him.

"Not tonight, pal," I whispered, speaking to Don's knob as though it were a microphone.

But then I wondered, why not . . . ?

As I held his warm prick in my hand, feeling it pulse between my fingers, I began gently stroking it, and it grew even more. I touched his balls, and they became tight. I could have straddled him, rubbing the head of his dick between my labia and across my clit. His cock could have been the best vibrator there was. I could have fucked him; I could have done almost anything. The only thing that was impossible was for Don to lick my cunt.

If I stared wanking him, would he wake up? Could I give him an orgasm while he remained unconscious? Somehow, it didn't seem fair to take advantage of him. I leaned closer towards Don's cock, smelling the potent aroma of his maleness, and I kissed the tip of the purple glans.

"Goodnight," I whispered.

I noticed my mouth had left a trace of lipstick on the virile flesh, and my tongue flickered out, licking it away. Then I undressed and got into bed. I took hold of his tool in my left hand, and caressed my cunt with my right. But I was too tired even to masturbate myself, and I soon fell asleep.

Always a light sleeper, the next morning I was awake as soon as Don began to stir. It took him a while before he was fully awake, and from the corner of my eye I saw him staring at me. He kept completely still for a while, trying not to wake me, but the covers moved as he reached down and discovered he was naked. He reached for his glasses and then slowly, ever so slowly, he raised the blankets to find out if I were similarly nude. I was. He let the covers fall back into place. He looked totally confused, and I had a lot of difficulty in not laughing; but at least the top sheet covered my smile.

Carefully, Don eased himself out of bed. I studied his naked body. He was incredibly thin, and his dick was once again like that of a child. Rubbing at his head, evidently still affected by the previous night's consumption of alcohol, he headed for the basin in the corner of the room. He turned on the cold tap, removed his glasses and pushed his face beneath the flow of water.

"Good morning," I said.

He spun around swiftly, grabbing a towel to hold in front of his crotch.

"Hi!" he responded, peering towards me. He put his glasses back on. "How are you?"

I smiled, sitting up. "How do you think?" And I allowed the covers to drop away and expose my breasts.

"Er . . ."

That was the first and only time I've known Don to be lost for words.

I kept looking at him, waiting for his next response. It was obvious he couldn't remember. He knew something must have happened last night, and from the circumstances it could only have been one thing. But without any memory of the event, that left him at a severe disadvantage. His eyes moved from my tits towards his clothes on the floor, then back again, as he desperately tried to remember. Then he shook his head.

"Nothing happened," he said.

"You call that nothing?" I shook my head. "If so, I'd like to know what you call something."

"I drank too much last night. I couldn't possibly have . . . . er . . ."

I raised my forearm and clenched my fist in the ancient phallic gesture, and Don nodded.

"Ha!" I laughed.

I pushed the bedcovers aside and stood up, totally nude, and walked towards Don. He gazed at me, eyes wide.

"What's the matter?" I asked. "You've seen me before."

He ran his fingers through his short black hair, not sure what to believe, his drunken memory or the evidence of his own eyes.

"That was a great night," I told him, and I kissed his cheek. "Thanks." I reached behind the towel and found his cock, giving it an affectionate squeeze. "Thank you both."

I walked back, picked up my clothes from the chair by the bed, and began dressing.

"Er . . . can't we do it again?" Don suggested. He hung the towel up. His cock was also beginning to show interest in me.

"Some other time," I said. "We aren't here to enjoy ourselves, are we? What about that thousand line free form verse about the migration of Peruvian geese scheduled for this morning?"

He nodded. "Can't miss that, I suppose."

Ever since then Don had been trying to get me into bed again – or just into bed. We had become good friends, although as time went by he'd become less convinced that anything had happened between us. There was always a fraction of doubt, however, whereas I knew exactly what had happened . . . or hadn't.

We saw each other frequently because we had so much in common. What we did ran in parallel, and so we always had a lot to discuss. That evening in the pub was no exception, and we started by talking about what all writers did: editors and agents, how they were always so s-l-o-w. It was just nice to be with someone who understood my way of life; and I knew the same was true of Don.

That, however, wasn't the only reason I had wanted to talk with him.

"I wanted to ask you about doing some other kind of work," I said, when he came back with my second drink. He was still only a few sips into his first.

"Very wise." He nodded thoughtfully. "Have you ever thought of becoming a secretary? What about an airline stewardess? Or a nurse?"

"You know what I mean," I said, flicking some beer at him. The drops coated one lens of his glasses. "Some other kind of writing. The sort you do."

"Write a film? Well," he shook his head, "I don't know if the movie world is big enough for the two of us."

"You know," I repeated, and I flicked more beer at him, onto the other lens, "what I mean."

Don polished his glasses on his sleeve. "Men write for men's magazines. Women write for men's magazines."

"But men's magazines are about women. They call them girlie mags, don't they? I'm a girlie."

"I wouldn't dare call you one."

"I could write that kind of thing."

Don replaced his glasses and stared at me. "What kind of thing?"

I took a mouthful of my drink. "I was hoping you'd tell me that." I smiled. "And if you ever want to write for a woman's magazine, I'll tell you all you need to know."

"Sounds fair enough to me," he agreed, and he smiled wryly. "I suppose you'd also want me to mention your name to a few editors I know?"

"Of course."

"You're so good to me."

"I know."

For the first time in a while, Don took a sip from his glass. "You're right, men's magazines are all about women – or 'girls' as they are known in the trade. Most of the pages are filled with photos of undressed ladies. And they have to fill the pages between the photo spreads, so there are various features about sex. Letters, articles, that sort of stuff. But no fiction."

"Isn't is all fiction?"

"Yeah, but it isn't written as fiction; it's all written as true confessions. There are also humorous articles, which must have something to do with sex. You can easily recognise these because they aren't funny, whereas the other stuff often is – although it isn't meant to be."

"You write both kind of things?"

"Yeah, but my funny stuff is funny."

"Such as?"

Don shrugged. "You can find a sex angle for anything. Suggest something."

"Computers," I said, thinking of the most boring subject I could imagine.

Don took yet another sip of his beer. "Software and hardware," he said, nodding, as though that was answer enough. When I made no response, he continued, "Soft equals female, hard equals male. Get it? Or a cock becoming erect. Software becoming hardware."

"You're just too subtle for me, Don," I sighed.

"Office technology. Bosses and secretaries. Switchboard girls and extensions. The bank rate, the rate at which bankers fuck. Mergers."

"Industrial relations," I said.

"Yeah." Don nodded.

"Trade unions."

"Yeah, yeah." He nodded twice.

I could almost see him making a mental note of what we were saying. He'd probably go straight home and write it all up.

"I think I'd better leave that sort of thing to the experts," I told him. "What about the other stuff?"

"Yeah. 'I fucked her' or 'he fucked me.'"

"Just like that."

"In more detail than that if it's as a letter to the editor. Or in a lot more detail if it's as part of a series of articles." Don watched me for several seconds, then asked, "Are you sure that's what you want to write?"

I nodded. "It'll make a change. Maybe I could write about how I once took a drunk to bed with me, stripped him off and . . ." I sipped at my drink.

Don waited for me to continue. When I didn't, he said, "I think it's been done."

"Has it?"

"I seem to remember reading something like that a couple of years ago."

"Or writing it?"

He shrugged.

"What happened?" I asked. I was amused that Don had be inspired by the incident, intrigued to discover what he had written.

He scratched at his head, as if trying to remember. "There was this guy who went out for a few drinks with a really attractive blonde."

"Blonde?"

"The details might have been changed to protect the guilty. But she could have been a redhead, in fact I think she was. He thought she was terrific, very good company, intelligent, amusing. And really wanted to fuck her, but he knew he stood no chance. So what he did was pretend to get drunk, very drunk. Because they were staying at the same hotel, the girl took him back. She couldn't find which room the guy was in, so she took him into hers. Once there, she stripped off all the guy's clothes, then her own. She thought he was totally oblivious to what she did to him, but he wasn't. He knew exactly what was happening."

"Which was?" I asked.

"You tell me your version first."

I smiled. "A secret."

"How about a repeat performance?" Don lifted his glass to his lips, draining it in a few gulps. "I'll pretend to get drunk again. We go back to my place. Or yours. And . . ."

"And?"

"We take our clothes off, get into bed, et cetera."

"You're too much of a friend, Don. I can't fuck you."

"If you can't fuck a friend, who can you fuck?"

We both noticed how quiet it had become, that the people sitting at the nearby tables had all turned to stare at us. We looked at each other, and we both burst out laughing.

At least that saved me having to come up with an answer, because it was a very good question: could I like someone too much to fuck them . . . ?

"Want another drink?" I asked, emptying my own glass.

"Will it do me any good?" he asked.

"It won't get your hardware into my software."

"But we could collaborate so well." Don exhaled loudly, then shook his head. "You really want to write some sex stuff?"

"Yes. I want to do something different."

"Here's a name," said Don, taking out his pen and writing on the corner of one of the sheets of paper in front of him, "and a phone number. I've known Jeff for a while, and for an editor he's almost honest. He's worth getting in touch with because he's starting up a new magazine, and he needs writers. I'll phone him tomorrow, mention your name. He wants ideas for new material. He asked me, but with Hollywood calling . . ."

"Thanks, Don."

We got up and left the bar. We kissed goodbye, chastely, but on the lips.

"What about a wank?" said Don.

"If you want," I told him. "Go into that alley, and I'll keep watch till you've finished."

He sighed, then smiled. "I'll have to put myself in the hands of an expert," he said, raising his right hand. "See you." He waved goodbye, then turned away.

"Be seeing you." I watched him walk down the road, then I headed off in the opposite direction.

'What happened to me last week was so fantastic that I have to tell someone. And for reasons which will become evident I can't tell my wife and neither can I tell my best friend, so I am writing this letter instead.

My wife, Jane, was visiting her sister for the weekend and had left me to look after myself. I came home from work on Friday, made myself some coffee, then discovered there was no milk in the refrigerator. So I went next door to borrow some milk. My next door neighbour is Terry, who is also my best mate. We've known each other ever since we were kids. A year after Jane and I were married and moved

27

into our new house, the house next door came up for sale. Terry bought it and moved in with his new bride, Sonia. The two girls became close friends too, and would go shopping together or stay in to watch a video whenever Terry and I saw a match or went out drinking.

I knocked on the back door, but when there was no reply I tried the door handle. "Terry!" I called, as I entered the kitchen. Terry should have been home by now, and there must have been someone in or the door would not have been unlocked.

"Sonia!" I yelled, when there was no response. I waited a while longer, then yelled, "Hello!"

"Hello, Pete," said a voice behind me, and I spun around as Sonia entered the kitchen. All she wore was a short towelling robe, which she was fastening around her waist.

"Terry phoned to say he was working late," she said, "so I was grabbing a few minutes on the sun bed. Is there anything I can help you with?"

Dressed like that, there was a lot she could have helped me with. Sonia has long blonde hair, and her shapely legs seemed even longer, her firm breasts even bigger, because of the brevity of her white robe. I'd frequently admired her exquisite body, having caught sight of her sunbathing in a tiny bikini which could hardly contain the contours of her ripe body. She was my best friend's wife, however, definitely taboo – but that hadn't stopped me fancying her like crazy.

"Milk," I said hurriedly. "I've made some coffee and there's no milk."

"Is that all?" she laughed. "Sure I can't tempt you with something else?"

"What?"

"Beer? Wine? Gin?"

28

"Ah!" I laughed, then shook my head. "Milk will be fine, thanks."

Sonia walked to the refrigerator. The belt around her waist was very loose, and I could see the inner curves of her tanned breasts as she moved close by me. She noticed the direction of my gaze and she pulled the edges of her robe closer together, but she smiled as she did so. She opened the fridge door and leaned down. The hem of the towelling robe had been only an inch or two below her bottom. But as she bent over, the fabric began to rise up over her buttocks.

I gasped in amazement at the gorgeous sight of what Sonia had inadvertently revealed. But a moment later I realised that this was no accidental exposure. She had deliberately bent from the waist in order to display her bare behind. Her legs were parted, and at the top of her thighs I could even make out a few wisps of pubic hairs. I had often wondered if Sonia was a genuine blonde, and now I knew that she was.

By now, needless to say, I had a massive hard-on . . .

"Is there anything else you want while I'm here?" asked Sonia.

Her bum still in the air, she was gazing at me from between her legs, her face upside down. She grinned when she saw me unzip my flies. I stepped closer, hearing her gasp with pleasure as my eight-inch tool sprang free of its denim prison.

Sonia thrust her inviting buttocks towards me, and they still felt hot from the rays of her sunlamp. I slid my rock-hard rod down between her buttocks, and I felt her hands clutch my own bum, urging me on. I pushed the head of my knob against her quim, which was already wet, then slid my piston straight into her tight pussy.

"Ohhh . . . ," she moaned. "Fuck me, fuck me!"

I did as Sonia requested, and she climaxed almost immediately, shrieking out her triumph.

We fucked on the kitchen floor. We fucked on the sofa in the lounge. We fucked upstairs on the bed. Then we took a shower together, where we fucked again.

I never did get my milk, but Sonia certainly had my cream!'

Before heading home, I stopped at a newsstand and studied the glossy array of voluptuous boobs and curvaceous bums which adorned the men's magazines. If I intended to write for them, I ought to find out exactly what it was that they published. It was difficult to know which to buy. I should have asked Don, but it was too late now. They cost a lot more than the women's magazines, I discovered. The cover girls seemed almost interchangeable. They wore very little, if anything, although nipples and groins were covered by skimpy underwear, a modest hand or a strategically placed item. And all the titles were similarly similar, so I chose half a dozen at random.

It felt a little strange buying that kind of material, and I tried to imagine the reverse situation: a man buying half a dozen women's magazines. What would he want them for? His fix on romance and royalty, cookery and crocheting?

The man took my money, and he didn't blink an eye. As long as I paid, he didn't care.

I went home via the Chinese takeaway, and resisted opening the magazines until I'd eaten. Then I opened the first of them and read the first letter.

Pete's amorous encounter with Sonia was typical. There were dozens more "letters from readers" like that in the other magazines, or longer versions which purported to be "confessions" or "interviews". A variation on this would be a query to the magazine's advice columnist, who was always a beautiful nude girl.

Pete, for example, would have concluded his letter by asking, 'Terry is still by best friend, but should I keep on fucking his wife?'

And the reply would be, 'You should stop before he gets home! But seriously, I wish I was Sonia and had a neighbour like you!'

I had a very interesting night studying what I'd bought. I'd encountered such publications previously, but this was the first time I had paid them very much attention – because, after all, they weren't aimed at me.

But I found myself in a world where every man was a virile stud, every woman an insatiable nymphomaniac and spermaholic. Every cock was at least eight inches long, and all the women had huge breasts and seldom wore bras. Most of them had long blonde hair too, which wasn't much different from romantic fiction.

Every girl would drop her knickers at the sight of a cock, as though it were a magic wand, and every orgasm was magnified into a multiple climax.

Sex always occurred almost immediately. Strangers would meet and fuck. Nurses gave blowjobs with bedbaths. Every hitcher was a nubile teenager, and they were always screwed by the brawny truck drivers who picked them up. Male/female lecturers routinely fucked and sucked their female/male students.

But this was only exaggeration, a condensation of reality, of cutting out the unnecessary formalities.

The same was true with any work of art. In movies, Westerns focused on the shootouts; thrillers concentrated on the chases. It was the action, the excitement, which was the true core. Everything else was extraneous. That was why foreign films were so boring, despite all the sex and nudity, because of the longueurs between the fucking.

Sex was the most important thing in the world, the most vital in the universe. Without it none of us would be here, without it there would be no future.

It was also the most important thing to write about, and the only thing worth writing about.

After my exhaustive study of the magazines, I knew that I could do it – and also that I wanted to.

But, as Don had said, the words were only there to fill in the pages between the nude models.

Although I'd seen such pictures before, these seemed far more explicit than any I'd previously encountered. Perhaps I hadn't paid that much attention because I was never very interested, but until now I'd assumed that a nude picture was simply that: a picture of a nude girl. Yet all of those featured in the magazines were far more than simply nude.

Imagine a girl with clothes, then remove those clothes. What do you see that was previously hidden? Her breasts and her crotch, and the crotch is covered by pubic hair.

Not, however, in the case of a magazine nude, where the whole idea was to make sure that her crotch was not covered by anything. The girls were posed in such positions that their cunts were the focal point of the majority of pictures. They lay on their backs, their legs spread; they knelt on their hands and knees, their thighs parted. They were ready to be fucked.

I found myself studying numerous twats in extreme close-up, often shaven so that no intimate detail could possibly be

32

hidden. Often they were larger than life-size, with succulent pink labia and clits that glistened.

And all of the models had names as exotic as those found in romantic fiction. The one who had caught my attention was Jasmine. Instead of the sultry pout which most of the girls essayed, she was biting her lower lip, trying to hide her smile. She knew she was there just for the fun of it. And if she was enjoying what she did, then so was I.

By now, I had taken the magazines to bed to read. It was still sweltering hot, and I was lying naked on top of the covers – although not as naked as the all-revealing girls in the magazine. Stimulated by everything I had read, I realised my clit and my cunt lips were as swollen as Jasmine's.

Each girl who was featured in the magazines had several pages devoted to her, and there would usually be a few paragraphs of text to accompany the photographs.

'We asked Jasmine to talk about herself, and she said:

I like good food, good conversation, good movies, and good fucking. But not necessarily in that order.

I like a man who will take me to a restaurant where they appreciate the art of cooking; but if I am on my own, I can microwave a pizza.

I like a man who can debate politics and philosophy, economics and ecology; but if I am on my own, I can talk to the cat.

I like a man who knows the right movie for us to see, the height of European culture; but if I am on my own, I can watch a soap on television.

I like a man who can give me a thorough shafting, who knows when to treat me as a lady, when to treat me as a tramp; but if I am on my own . . .

We watched as Jasmine licked the index and middle

fingers of her right hand, slipping them down between her thighs. She began rubbing her hand up and down, smiling as she did so. Whatever it was that she was doing, it seemed that she was not paying much attention to us, and so we made an excuse and left.'

And some of the things in the magazines were not exaggerated at all, I realised, as I licked the index and middle finger of my right hand, slipping them down between my thighs, rolling my clitoris between my knuckles and thrusting my fingers between my labia.

THREE

Exhausted by the thorough finger-fucking I'd given myself the previous night, I was still half-asleep when the phone rang.

"Hi!" said Don.

"Huh," I yawned.

"Get you up, did I?"

"Uh-huh."

"Well, you always get me up . . ."

"What?" I muttered.

"Never mind. Listen, I just phoned Jeff, the editor I spoke to you about last night. Remember? He's very interested in what you can do, and he's expecting you to call him."

"Right, uh, thanks. I will. Er, how's things?"

"Not much different from last night."

I remembered last night and wondered if Don had been tossing himself off while I had been making myself come. Why did we always part when we should have done the exact opposite?

"What about you?" Don continued, asking another question before I could think of an answer to my own. "What are you doing today?"

"I've got to see an editor," I told him, and I glanced at the clock. "There isn't time to talk, Don, I must get dressed."

"You mean you're in the nude?"

"That's right. You're talking to a naked girl."

"Ahhhh," he sighed. "Wait a moment, let me get my clothes off too."

"Idiot!" I laughed. "I'll phone you, let you know what happens with Jeff."

I hung up, then moved cautiously across the room. The two workmen on the scaffolding were still there, still apparently doing nothing. It looked as hot and humid outside as it had been for the past several days. I took a shower and washed my hair.

The other phone call I had made yesterday afternoon had been to Stephanie, the editor who had asked me for the Samantha/Jeremy story. I'd told her that it was finished and would be mailed within an hour.

"Save yourself a stamp," she had told me. "Why don't you bring it in tomorrow? It's my birthday, and I'm having lunch with some friends from work."

I'd hoped Stephanie would invite me out, which was why I had phoned, but I told her I wasn't sure I wanted to intrude if it was her birthday.

"No, I'd love you to be there," she had said. "It's girls only, and the more the better. One o'clock?"

I'd agreed, and while I fixed my make-up I wondered what to put on. It was too hot to wear very much. When there were guys there, they always looked at my tits, and to their simple minds going without a bra seemed to mean "let's fuck"; but at least today there would be no such problem – except on the way across the city.

Trying on my white silk blouse, which was edged with lace, I remembered why I wore it so rarely: it was translucent, and my nipples could be seen through the thin fabric. That was solved by wearing a red velvet waistcoat over the top, which would also prevent my boobs bouncing up and down too much as I walked.

That was half of my outfit decided. Naked below the waist,

I went through my wardrobe trying to find the other half of my ensemble. I pulled on a pair of white cotton briefs, then kept searching. There were some red denims which would have matched my waistcoat – and my hair – but it would be far too hot to wear anything so tight around my legs. I made do with a black skirt; the hem hung just above my knees. Red suede sandals completed my outfit. Putting the manuscript in my shoulder bag, I headed off into the city.

"Happy birthday," I said to Stephanie. "Here's your present."

I gave her my manuscript and she smiled, dropping the envelope on top of the pile of papers on her desk.

"Thanks."

She would get around to reading the story eventually. I knew it was the kind of thing she would publish, because it was so similar to the other material of mine which she had bought. If there was anything she didn't like, she would alter it. Editors always found something to alter, because that was their job.

"You ready to party?" she asked, picking up her phone.

"Always ready," I told her.

Stephanie was about thirty, petite, with delicate features. I had no idea what colour her hair was, because it was different every time I saw her. This month it was jet black, cut very short.

"Is Beth with you?" she asked. "Good. Round up the others, and we'll see you downstairs in two minutes." She replaced the receiver.

"Beth?" I said. "The illustrator?"

Stephanie nodded. "You know everyone who's coming. Five more who work here, plus me. And because of Beth and you we can claim it all on expenses!"

Beth had done the illustrations for many of my stories. She was very good on square-jawed heroes and exotic landscapes, although her heroines always seemed far too similar. I realised why the first time I met Beth: all her heroines looked like her. Blonde, brunette or redhead, long-haired or short, she always modelled the protagonists' facial features upon her own. In person, Beth was always smartly clad in matching skirt and jacket, like some businesswoman. It was as if she had to go to an office every day, whereas those who worked on the magazine dressed far more casually than she did.

Eight of us headed off to celebrate Stephanie's birthday. The other five were Carla, Meg, Karen, Rachel and Susie. Carla was the one who had made the arrangements, and she led the way down the road, across the street, and around the corner into an Italian restaurant. The waiter led us into a private dining room, where a huge table was waiting, and we took our seats. I was to Stephanie's left, Beth to her right.

"Eight bottles of vino," said Carla, "four white, four red."

"So what's Ronnie given you for your birthday?" asked Karen. Ronnie was the guy who Stephanie lived with.

Stephanie merely smiled. She pushed the tip of her tongue between her lips, slowly thrusting it out, then wiggling it up and down lasciviously.

"No wonder you've looked so happy all morning!" said Susie.

"If that's what you get, I can't wait for my birthday!" Carla said, and everyone laughed.

The waiter returned, pushing a trolley laden with wine bottles. He was in his mid-thirties, tall and lean. With a great deal of bowing and smiling, he uncorked all the bottles and moved around the table filling the glasses.

"Nice bum," remarked Meg, gazing at the waiter's taut backside. She leaned back in her chair to examine his rear, and her palm followed the contours of the waiter's buttocks, not quite touching him. He spilled wine onto the table as he straightened up hurriedly.

"I often have that effect on men," Meg sighed, and there was more laughter.

We started to drink the wine, to study the menu, and all the time there were at least three conversations going on at once. We gave our orders, and the talking continued.

Rachel was to my left, and she was telling me about her recent holiday in Greece. I was very envious; I'd always wanted to see that part of the world.

"I don't believe you," I told her. "You got that suntan here, I bet, lying in the park."

"Oh, yeah?" she said. "An all-over tan in the park?" Then she unbuttoned her blouse and held it open to prove her tits were as tanned as the rest of her. She had no bikini lines around her bare breasts.

But I wasn't the only one who had seen the evidence. There was a huge crash as two laden dishes clattered to the floor. Our meal had arrived, although some of it had ended up on the ground.

There was another waiter with the first one, and he could only have been seventeen. It was he who had dropped the dishes, distracted by the sight of Rachel's blatant boobs, and he had gone red in the face. He bent down and began to pick up what he had dropped.

"Isn't he cute?" said Rachel, as she slowly covered her bare breasts and buttoned up her blouse. "Fresh young cock, nothing like it. Three times an hour at that age, no problem. But soon . . ." She shook her head wistfully.

39

She wasn't the only one watching the youth. "And doesn't teenage spunk taste better?" asked Meg, gazing at the waiter's crotch.

"Better than what?" asked Susie.

"Better than almost everything!" laughed Meg.

"You were on a nudist beach?" I asked Rachel, changing the subject.

She nodded, still gazing at the young waiter.

"Doesn't it feel odd being naked in front of strangers?" As I spoke, I remembered that I'd been naked in front of strangers only the day before, when the two workmen had seen me.

"It's easier being naked in front of strangers than people you know," said Rachel. "Apart from lovers, of course. But I wouldn't let the guys in the office see me in the nude, for example."

I nodded, understanding what she meant, and I poured us both some more wine. The two waiters began to serve the meal. The older one made a great fuss of us all, but it was the younger one who was the centre of attention. He could hardly understand English, which made him even more popular.

"Can I sit on your face?" asked Carla.

"Si, Signorina," he replied, nodding.

"You like to eat pussy?" asked Susie.

"Si, Signorina," he replied, again.

For the time being it was only the meal which was consumed, and finally the dishes were removed. More and more wine flowed, which was directly proportional to the conversations becoming louder and lewder, until they were finally silenced by Carla banging a spoon against the side of her glass.

"I suppose you're all wondering why I invited you here

today," she began. She waited until there was silence again, then continued, "Today is the birthday of our dear friend and colleague, Stephanie. I'm sure we could all tell many interesting and intimate stories about Steph, but in order to maintain some level of decorum and also not to embarrass her, we won't!"

"Tell us!" yelled Meg.

"Yes!" agreed Susie. "The one about the donkey!"

"Don't exaggerate," said Carla.

"Okay, the corgi," said Susie.

"Or when she was trapped in the lift with the messenger boy for an hour!" suggested Karen.

"A lie!" Stephanie retorted. "It was only half an hour!"

"Or the reason her dress was on back-to-front halfway through last year's Christmas party!" volunteered Karen.

"No, no," said Carla, shaking her head. "None of it would be fair." Then she shrugged. "But who wants to be fair . . . ?" The laughter increased.

"Carla . . . !" Stephanie warned, and the laughter multiplied.

"We're all friends here," Carla told her. "We've all done things we'd rather forget. The only difference is: we won't let you forget . . ."

Stephanie smiled but she gripped her empty wine glass, wondering what indiscretion Carla was about to reveal. Carla swirled the last of her wine in her glass, then swallowed it.

"But first," announced Carla, snapping her fingers. "Champagne!"

A cheer went up, although I didn't add to the chorus. I felt as though I'd already drunk far too much. Alcohol always affected me more at lunchtime than in the evening, and yet the prospect of champagne was very enticing.

As if he had been awaiting Carla's signal, the waiter

41

pushed in a trolley laden with ice-buckets, each silver bucket containing bottles of genuine French champagne. It was a different waiter, I noticed, and he didn't seem very Italian. His hair was fair, his complexion pale.

That was not the only thing which was unusual about him, because to open the first bottle of champagne he held it between his thighs while he untwisted the wire from the cork. Most of the others at the table were trying not to laugh, and I realised there was something going on that I didn't know about. Stephanie was watching him in astonishment.

"You lika taste?" he asked her, in what was an obviously fake Italian accent.

The bottle jutted blatantly from his crotch, and he stroked its neck with his left hand while he unfastened the wire. The cork suddenly exploded from the bottle, and champagne foamed from the top.

The girls from the office cheered, and the waiter filled Stephanie's glass first. He began filling the other glasses, then opened another bottle, this time in a more conventional manner.

"To Stephanie!" cried Carla, raising her glass.

"Stephanie!" we all echoed, as we joined in the toast.

I took a mouthful of champagne, the bubbles tickling my mouth and throat. There was nothing like it.

"Thank you," said Stephanie, and she lifted her own glass. She glanced at the waiter for a moment, who was opening another bottle in the orthodox method, then said, "To my friends." And she also drank.

"For da bella Senorita," said the waiter, as he refilled her glass.

Stephanie looked at him again. Senorita? "Gracias," she said.

"Cheers," he replied, and he raised the champagne bottle to his lips and took a swig. Then he leaned down to the bottom shelf of the trolley, which was hidden by the white cloth.

By now most of the others had given up trying to hide their laughter, and I wondered what the joke was.

"We bought you a birthday present, Steph," said Carla.

Then there was a sudden blare of music, a loud disco beat. There must have been a ghetto-blaster on the wine trolley. The waiter jumped up, grinning, and began to dance.

Stephanie stared at him. "Oh no," she groaned.

"Oh yes!" said a chorus of voices.

Stephanie sank lower in her chair, then took a deep swallow of champagne.

"This is Marvin," said Carla.

The dancing waiter paused in his routine to bow, but it was only when he removed his jacket, used it as an imaginary dancing partner and then and draped it around Stephanie's shoulders that I realised what was going on: he was a stripper!

Stephanie had her hand over her face, pretending not to look, but making it evident that she was doing so. The others were all laughing, cheering, clapping, calling out ribald remarks. I could understand now why we had been given a room to ourselves.

"More, more!" someone chanted.

"No, less, less!" someone else countered.

I watched, amazed. I'd never seen a male stripper before; and I'd only seen female ones in movies. My heart began to beat faster as he began to peel off his uniform, and the more he removed the faster it became. It was almost if he were undressing for me, that we were alone together.

Marvin had kicked his shoes away as he danced, his waistcoat was gone and he slowly unbuttoned his white shirt to the waist. Stephanie had pushed his jacket from her shoulders to the floor, and he beckoned to her, trying to persuade her to her dance with him. Instead she reached for an unopened champagne bottle. It was evident that half of the others would willingly have danced with Marvin, but he was Stephanie's present and so they restrained themselves – if it could be called restraint . . .

Barefoot, he sprang up on the table, and a moment later he had his shirt off. He danced around the glasses, waving his shirt like a matador's cloak, advancing towards Stephanie and then retreating.

The champagne cork flew off, and she filled her glass and mine, which I had drained without noticing. "What did I do to deserve friends like these?" she asked, trying hard not to smile.

Marvin threw his shirt over her head, and she swept it away very quickly because it had been obstructing her view.

I noticed Beth had her sketchpad out, and she was drawing very quickly, gazing up at the dancer for a moment, then down at what she was doing.

All Marvin was wearing now was his pair of tight black trousers – and his black bow-tie. He swung his hips from side to side in rhythm with the music, then jerked them back and forth. The latter proved more popular with the majority of his audience, who demonstrated their approval even more vocally.

"Get 'em off!"

"Get 'em down!"

"Get it up!"

"Get it in!"

44

He reached for the button on his waistband, flicking it open with his thumb. There was a cheer as it came undone. He danced over the table, back to Stephanie, thrusting his hips at her, gesturing towards his zip. He lowered himself towards her, getting ever nearer. His crotch was at the same level as her face, and she leaned away.

"Don't be shy," Marvin told her.

"Pull it down, Steph!"

"Pull it out!"

Marvin shrugged and turned slightly, so that his zip was directly in front of me. He beckoned with his fingers. I clutched my glass with both hands, managing to resist the urge to reach out and tug down the clasp. Marvin next turned to Rachel, who made as if to unzip him, then pulled back, laughing.

"Nobody?" he said. "I don't believe it!"

"Over here, Marv," said Carla, and she waved her arms in time to the beat. "Try my hand."

"I'd rather try your . . ." began Marvin, moving towards her.

"What?" asked Carla, and she yanked down his zip.

"What you got?" asked Marvin.

"What you got?" asked Carla, and she slipped her hand inside the zip.

She wasn't fast enough, and Marvin evaded her grasp, moving quickly backward, spinning around and allowing his trousers to fall around his ankles, then kicking them away. The cheer was the loudest yet as he was left standing in a pair of baggy shorts. They were bright green, with a row of buttons down each hip.

I thought that was the end of the show, but I was wrong. Surely Marvin wouldn't show more, couldn't show more. But he kept on dancing on the table, and the others were all gazing eagerly up at him, still cheering and leering. Was he going to take off everything . . . ?

He returned to Stephanie, thrusting his left hip towards her, running his fingers up and down the buttons. At last she responded, reaching up. But before she could touch the first button, Marvin had retreated again. He blew her a kiss. But as he backed away, Susie quickly stretched out her right arm and tugged at the hem of his pants, dragging them down a few inches before he could jump away. I saw blond public hairs curling above the waistband, and then Marvin managed to pull his shorts back into place.

"Boo!"

"Hiss!"

"Cheat!"

His audience jeered, obviously only liking the strip, not the tease. But then he went around the table, letting everyone undo the buttons, while he kept his hands on his hips, holding the garment up. There were enough buttons for us all, but a few of the girls were greedy, tearing eagerly at them. Within seconds each side of Marvin's pants was completely undone. I felt oddly cheated that I hadn't taken part in Marvin's ritual strip. He stopped and looked around at us.

"Thank you, ladies," he said. "And goodbye."

There was silence for a moment, except for the ghetto-blaster which was still blaring away.

"What?" demanded Carla.

I was right. Marvin hadn't removed his shorts. But I was only right for another split second, because then he leapt into the air, hurling the bright green fabric away.

There was more cheering, even though he wasn't naked. He was clad in a white leather posing pouch, which was framed by a mass of fair curls. The garment was almost moulded to the contours of his genitals, and it was patently evident that Marvin was a big boy. The leather was held in place by a thong between his bare buttocks, tied around his waist.

Surely, I thought as he kept on dancing, as the others kept on applauding in time to the music, he wouldn't remove that . . .

Marvin's dance became even more blatant, thrusting his crotch back and forth as though he were fucking. There was a great roar of approval from those on the other side of the table, and I didn't understand why until he turned. The tip of his cock had worked itself free from the side of the pouch!

"It's alive!" screamed Karen, and she threw her glass of champagne at his crotch.

"Don't waste the bubbly!" yelled Meg. She stood up and leaned towards Marvin, thrusting her tongue towards his prick and the drops of champagne upon it. Then she pulled back and laughed, as though she had only been kidding. But I knew it had been more than a joke.

"You want it?" said Marvin. "Come and get it." He gestured to his hips, where the thong was fastened.

He didn't need to ask twice. My hands were amongst those which reached up. Only Stephanie sat still, and Beth kept on sketching. I wasn't fast enough. In an instant the fastenings were ripped away, the pouch was gone, and Marvin was totally naked.

Or almost. He still had on his bow-tie, and there were what seemed to be two uninflated balloons tied around his cock – and also a pink ribbon.

"A dickie-bow!" shouted someone.

Perhaps the dimensions I had read in the magazines were

47

not exaggerated. Marvin's cock seemed very long, very thick, although it was difficult to judge after the amount of alcohol I'd swallowed – and also because he kept swinging it from side to side, up and down. But I supposed that penis size was important in his profession.

"You've got to unwrap your gift, Steph!" called Carla.

Stephanie glanced at Beth, who was too busy drawing. She glanced at me, and she sighed. But she was smiling as she did so. She raised her right hand and beckoned to Marvin with her index finger. He danced down to our end of the table, his cock jiggling as if it had a life of its own. Stephanie reached towards the pink ribbon, and Marvin danced back.

"No hands!" he said.

Stephanie frowned, not understanding. Then, as realisation came, she shook her head and cried, "No!"

"Come on!"

"Be a sport!"

"Bet you've done it before!"

Stephanie looked at Beth, and this time Beth returned her gaze.

"Don't you dare sketch this!" she warned. She took a mouthful of champagne, wiped her lips with the back of her hand, then stood up and put her hands around her back.

Marvin advanced again, his wriggling dick at the same height as Stephanie's waiting mouth – although it wasn't his cock she was awaiting, but the ribbon, or at least in theory. She had to remove the ribbon using just her teeth. The laughter and the jokes, the cheers and the noise were louder than ever.

Stephanie's task would have been much simpler if Marvin had remained still, or if one particular part of his anatomy had ceased moving. But his tool kept on rocking from side to side, slapping against her cheeks and rubbing across her lips.

"Keep still or I'll bite your balls!" she threatened.

"Promises, promises," replied Marvin, but he allowed his swaying knob to slow down.

Managing to catch the end of the ribbon between her teeth, Stephanie pulled. The ribbon came free, levering Marvin's cock upwards and poking her between the eyes. She sat down, triumphantly waving her trophy above her head.

"Who's going to give me a blowjob?" Marvin asked, gesturing to the balloons which dangled from his genitals.

"Me! Me! Me!"

There was no shortage of offers. Marvin chose Rachel and Karen as the winners. This time hands were allowed, in order to steady the balloons as they were inflated; but I noticed how Rachel and Karen also managed a good grope of Marvin's prick and testicles while they blew up the balloons. They were given plenty of encouragement to go further.

"Give it a good lick!"

"Open your mouth, swallow it down!"

Marvin simply stood there grinning, and I couldn't remember when I'd last laughed so much.

Finally Marvin burst the balloons and that seemed to be the end of the performance. He was well applauded and about to climb down from the table when Carla spoke up.

"Just a moment," she said. "I asked for at least eight inches. I want to make sure we go our money's worth." And she produced a tape measure.

Marvin laughed. "Go ahead," he offered.

Carla leaned forward, measuring the length of his dick, from base to tip. "Six and a half," she announced.

49

Marvin tugged at his cock, stretching it out.

"Seven and a quarter," said Carla, and she shook her head.

"You want it bigger?" asked Marvin, now serious. When Carla nodded, he said, "It'll cost."

"Get out your money, girls," said Carla. "The show's not over yet."

Banknotes cascaded onto the table between Marvin's feet. He looked down at what was there, not moving. But then he did begin to move. Or a part of him did.

I had already wondered about his self-restraint. I'd never seen an adult penis remain limp for such a long time. In female company, I'd noticed, the naked dick does not stay down for long.

Marvin began to get an erection. He didn't touch himself. What he did was gaze at us all in turn, obviously conjuring up some erotic fantasy in order to make himself hard. And as his cock stiffened it also grew. The thick vein on its underside pulsed, engorging the swelling length with even more blood, raising it towards the vertical. His testicles, which had hung loose, now tightened.

There was no cheering now, just rapt attention as we studied the magnificent phallus which was displaying itself for us. That was the focus of our attention, the only part of Marvin which interested us. And it was as though it no longer belonged to him, but to us.

My nipples had hardened while the prick had been doing the same, and my cunt lips had become swollen and damp.

The same must have been true of all the other acolytes who were witnessing the ritual.

A pearl of liquid appeared at the tip of the purple crown. This time it could not be champagne. It oozed free and dripped down Marvin's male flesh.

He gestured to Carla, asking if she wished to verify his credentials, but she shook her head.

"Shall we continue, ladies?" he asked, and he smiled as he removed his bowtie and tied it around his manhood.

There could be no doubt it wasn't the new ribbon he was offering. It was Meg's hand which reached his upright knob first, her palm sliding up and down, pulling it towards her and her mouth. I glanced at my empty champagne glass, and an obscene thought crossing my mind.

"It's Steph's birthday," someone said. "He's her present."

Despite my excitement, I was also feeling very uncomfortable at this naked display of female lust and male sexuality. Was Stephanie going to be fucked on the table while we all watched?

At that time, my theory of sex was that it was something which happened between two people.

Two people of the opposite sex.

And without an audience.

I had a lot to learn – and before too long, I did . . .

I noticed Beth looking at me. She closed her sketchpad and stood up. I also rose. We headed towards the door, leaving the others to it.

"It's okay for them," said Beth. "They can stay here as long as they like. But we freelancers have to work for a living."

"Yeah," I agreed. I still felt both amused and aroused, but I was glad to be out of there.

"I was never any good at maths," added Beth, "but even I know that one prick wouldn't go far amongst eight of us. Too many hands, too many mouths, too many cunts." She grinned.

I glanced back. "I wonder where those two waiters are?"

Beth laughed. As we reached the door she pulled out her sketchpad. She had made half a dozen rapid drawings of Marvin. In the last three he was totally naked; and in the last of those he was blatantly erect.

"We won't be able to use this for your new story, I suppose?"

"No," I agreed.

But the final sketch would have been very suitable for what happened between Samantha and Jeremy afterwards, the part of the story I'd deleted from the computer.

The first thing I wrote for Jeff, I decided, would feature a character called Marvin. I'd have no trouble describing his cock.

FOUR

Two days later I headed back to the centre of the city, to meet Jeff for the first time. I'd waited until the day after Stephanie's amazing birthday lunch before phoning him, partly because I hadn't wanted to seem too eager, partly because I'd been far too drunk to talk the day before.

"I'm very glad you got in touch," said Jeff. "Don recommended your work very highly, and I think we should meet as soon as possible. How about lunch tomorrow?"

"Fine," I said, wondering if I could face another editorial lunch so soon.

"Good. I'm supposed to be seeing someone else, but I'll cancel. Meeting writers is much more important."

We arranged a rendezvous, which left me with the problem of what to wear. Arranging to see a male editor was like going on a blind date, I supposed, although I had done neither before. What should I wear? But it was still too hot to wear much, and after going through my wardrobe I ended up in a skirt and blouse, but not the ones I had worn two days ago. The red skirt was neither too long nor too short, the white blouse neither too demure nor too revealing, and I wore a bra beneath. Bare-legged, shod in open-toe sandals, with my shoulder bag at my side, I set off for my appointment.

Arriving fifteen minutes early, I spent ten of those walking down the street then back again. The office was located in an old building which had been completely renovated within, and the receptionist on the ground floor phoned Jeff to say that I'd arrived.

"Take a seat," she told me. "He'll be down soon."

I sat, and looked through the magazines on the table in front of me. From the adverts displayed on the walls, it was evident that these were the company's publications. There were magazines about cameras and computers, cars and caravans . . . but nothing on cunts and cocksucking.

"Hi! I'm Jeff," said the man who approached me a few minutes later, smiling and offering his hand.

I stood up and we shook hands. He was in his mid-thirties, dressed in a dark suit. His hair and neatly trimmed beard were already beginning to turn grey. He had once been tall and lean, but was now beginning to spread around the middle.

"I've booked us a table at a Thai restaurant near here," he said. "You like Thai food?"

"As long as you're paying, I like anything."

Jeff laughed, and it sounded almost genuine. "I know exactly what you mean," he said, holding the door open for me. "I used to be a freelance. The only time I ever ate properly was when an editor took me out for a meal. And I always feel that taking out people like you is repaying that debt."

"So if and when I become an editor, I'll do the same?" I said.

"Exactly. But I often wish I still had the freedom of a freelance. Not having to come to the office every day, not having to wear a suit, not having to go to endless meetings with accountants, advertising executives. But it's nice to get paid regularly, I admit."

"It must be."

"If you do any work for me, I promise you will always be paid on time."

I nodded, although without any conviction, because it was impossible. The sun never rose in the west, winter never followed spring, and writers were never paid on time. Jeff might have meant what he said, but he wouldn't be the one who signed the cheques and put them in the post.

We went into the restaurant and were escorted to the table by the waiter, who handed a menu to me and the wine list to Jeff.

"A bottle of wine," Jeff asked me, "or something else?"

"Wine is alright by me," I said. "Order whatever you want."

He ordered without consulting the list. I studied the menu, not knowing whether I should be impressed or appalled by the prices. Jeff must have had a very lavish expense account, which probably accounted for his paunch. Once he had been a hungry writer, now he was a well-fed editor. I hoped this was also a sign that the magazine paid high fees for the material it published.

The waiter brought the wine, which was very smooth and inevitably very expensive. Jeff and I both ordered a starter and a first course. We could probably have flown to Thailand for the price of the meal.

"What did Don tell you about me?" asked Jeff.

"That you're a wonderful editor with exquisite taste," I replied.

"True." Jeff nodded seriously, then smiled. "About the magazine, I mean."

"Don just said that you were starting up a new magazine, that you needed writers, that you needed ideas."

"Right. Don has worked for me in the past. He's good, very good; he said that you were good, very good; and that's good enough for me."

"But I don't know if I can do what you want."

55

"Let me be the judge of that. A good writer can write about anything. As for what I want, we'll have to work that out between us. I know a lot of male writers, but very few female. We're producing a male-oriented magazine, but what I'd like is something from the female point of view."

I nodded, but said nothing. After what I'd read lately I could well imagine the kind of article that Jeff meant. Something from the female point of view would have a title like 'Fellatio: Does it Leave a Nasty Taste in your Mouth?'

"I was thinking of a regular column, maybe," Jeff continued. He swirled his wine around in his glass. "We could run your by-line every month, include your picture."

"I write under pseudonyms," I said. I was saving my real name for when my novels were published.

"That's okay. I used to have dozens of them myself."

I could well imagine the kind of monthly column that Jeff was considering. I'd read one or two of them recently. The narrator would write about her alleged sexual exploits the previous month: how she had fucked all the lads in a riding stable, or how she had licked out her flatmate's twat, or how she had sucked off the mechanic who had fixed her car. And such adventures were accompanied by detailed pictorial spreads – and it would be the girl's legs which did the spreading, her cunt which was detailed.

Writing them was one thing, but did Jeff seriously believe that I'd be willing to strip off and pose for such graphic illustrations?

"I am not going to take off my clothes and spread my legs," I told him.

Jeff stared at me, and he blinked. "Who asked you to? I'm a happily married man. You don't have to screw me to get into my magazine."

I looked at him, and he met my gaze. "I think we're talking about different things," I said.

"I think we are," he agreed, and he refilled our glasses. "I'm not editing a fuckzine. Don didn't tell you that?"

"No."

"Right, let's start again." He swallowed some wine. "It's a men's magazine, true, but it's more of a lifestyle publication. Articles on fashion, films, the arts, cars, more cars, interviews, features on business and politics. We can't have pictures of cunts – er, vaginas, I mean."

"Cunts, you mean," I said. "There's nothing wrong with the word 'cunt'."

"I know." He shrugged. "The magazine will be supported by adverts. Adverts for beer and spirits, for cigarettes and cars. And to get those sorts of adverts, we can't publish explicit photographs. There will be no nude features, not as such. In any case, we're aiming at a different market. We'll use nudes where appropriate, of course. Breasts are fine, even a flash of pubic hair now and then. Tasteful, arty stuff, but no more than that."

Now that Jeff had explained it to me, I wasn't sure whether to be disappointed or not, but I asked, "Where do I come in?"

"Well . . . there has to be some kind of sex angle, of course, there is in everything. To make the new magazine different I thought of using a female viewpoint, the kind of thing that only a woman could write, but which would be of interest to men."

I was right, Jeff did want articles like 'Fellatio: Is it Hard to Swallow?' I waited for him to continue.

"Men like reading about sex," he said, "and I'm not talking about fucking and sucking. I've always thought that was

57

something which should be done, not read about. But there are other aspects of sex. You thought I'd be editing a skin magazine, for example. To me, the most interesting part of such mags is the girls."

"Isn't that the idea?"

Jeff smiled. "I mean the real girls. Not the made up names, not the invented biographies. Who are they really? Why do they do it? What's it like to pose nude for pictures that will be seen by hundreds of thousands of men? That would make a good article, and probably only a woman could write it."

"And it would also give you a good excuse to run plenty of pictures of naked girls."

"Exactly. And it wouldn't be gratuitous because it would all be in context."

I looked at Jeff, but he managed to appear very serious. Then he took another sip of wine, perhaps to hide the smile which showed he knew he didn't mean it. The meal arrived and we began to eat.

"Good investigative journalism," Jeff said, "that's what I need."

It seemed that Jeff didn't need ideas for his magazine, he already knew the kind of thing he wanted me to write. A feature on glamour models was not what I would normally consider "investigative journalism', but he was the editor – and the best way to get anything published was to write what the editor wanted.

"I can do that," I told him, and I probably could.

"Good."

"And that's what you'd like, a piece on nude models?"

"Yes. We'll see how you do on that, then take it from there. This will be a trial assignment. I'm prepared to com- mission one piece from you, on spec. After that maybe you could have a regular feature in the magazine, under whatever pen-name you want. And without a photograph of you."

"How much?" I asked.

He told me, and it was more than I'd been paid for anything else. It was my turn to lift a wineglass to my lips to try and hide my expression. If I wrote for Jeff every month, I wouldn't need to do anything else. I would earn more than enough to live on, and I'd have time to write another novel.

"Sounds reasonable," I agreed.

"Plus expenses, of course."

"Of course."

"Another bottle of wine?" he suggested, emptying the first one into my glass.

"Yes," I said automatically. Already I was thinking beyond my first assignment. "So if this does become a regular feature, you want some aspect of sex each time? An interview, perhaps, or a behind-the-scenes article. Something which you can illustrate with provocative photos."

"Exactly." Jeff nodded for emphasis. "I knew as soon as I saw you that you were the right person for the job."

He continued studying me, and there was a different kind of look in his eye. He might have been happily married, but what difference did that make? He was male, I was female – and he wanted to fuck me.

I hoped that wasn't part of the job.

"Come in, take off your clothes, let's have a look at you."

"What?" I said.

The woman who had opened the door was dressed in a yellow running vest and matching shorts. She was in her mid-thirties, with shoulder-length ash blonde hair. Her name was Angela. She closed the door to her apartment behind me.

"I phoned you," I explained. "Don gave me your name."

"Ah, yes!" She nodded. "You don't look like a journalist."

"And you don't look like a photographer," I said, and we both smiled.

"I was expecting a new model an hour ago," said Angela. "But if it's their first time, they often don't arrive." She looked me up and down. "You're sure you don't want to take off your clothes?"

I shook my head.

Angela shrugged. "Would you like some tea?"

"Please."

"Make that three teas," she called.

She lived and worked above a row of shops in one of the older parts of the city. Her flat was at one end of the building, and she had taken over the adjacent apartments as her studio. We went through Angela's living area, past the dark-room, and into the studio. It must have been fifty feet long, divided up with all kinds of sets. There were several varieties of furniture, a small gymnasium, a whirlpool bath, and beds of every shape and size and design. The end nearest the apartment looked like part of a library, the corner walls lined with old books. The corner twenty feet opposite, however, had huge mirrors on either side. We sat down on an ancient sofa.

"Normally, I don't allow outsiders in here," said Angela, "but you were very persuasive."

When I'd asked Don for any contacts he had in the glamour world, I thought that he might have given me the names of a few girls who appeared in the magazines he wrote for.

"That's a completely different side of the business," he told me, when I explained what Jeff wanted me to write. "I don't know anything about the models. I don't even know any picture editors; they aren't the people I deal with."

"There must be someone you know who knows someone," I said. I was relying on him so that I could begin my first assignment.

"There's Angela," he said.

"She's a model?"

"She used to be, now she's a photographer. We work for the same magazines. I can get her number for you."

"You know her? Can I mention your name?"

"She might not know my name," Don had replied. "I only met her once. I was asked to write the captions for a series of pictures she'd taken; they were of a girl stripping off in a supermarket. She might remember, it was only a few months ago."

Angela had remembered. "The supermarket!" she laughed, when I phoned her.

My original intention had been to contact various models; but if Angela was an ex-model and now a photographer, I could probably write the whole article on her. Angela, however, hadn't been very enthusiastic when I suggested interviewing her. But when I said that I'd also need photographs of other girls, she became more keen. That was her profession, and she'd be paid for supplying illustrations. And so she had invited me to her studio.

"This is Dawn," said Angela, and I turned to see a tall girl carrying a tray laden with china cups and saucers, matching teapot, milk jug and sugar bowl.

She was naked.

Dawn was very shapely, with thick black hair which hung to her waist. I couldn't help stare – she was the first totally naked woman I had ever seen.

I'd lived a sheltered life, I have to admit. I went to a private school, and private meant privacy. Whenever we had a shower after sports, each girl had her own cubicle in which to shower, and another in which to change. Since then, there had never been any reason for me to see a naked woman. My friends and I hadn't been in the habit of stripping off in front of each other, and nor had I seen any unclad strangers. Unlike Rachel, I had never been to a nude beach. I'd seen Rachel's breasts last week, and I'd encountered several pairs of bare boobs in my time under various circumstances. A totally naked girl, however, was something different.

"I think your friend called her Charlotte," said Angela.

"Charlotte?" I repeated, my attention totally focused on Dawn's beautiful body. I tried not to stare at the fullness of her breasts, at the pinkness of her nipples, at the dark triangle of pubic hair at her crotch.

"When he wrote about the supermarket. Remember that afternoon, Dawn?"

Dawn laughed. She set the tray on a lacquered table in front of Angela and me, then sat down opposite us. "That was a lot of fun," she said. She tossed back her mane of jet black hair, and her breasts bounced.

She seemed totally oblivious of the fact that she was naked. She was a model, she was used to being in the nude, and so it meant nothing to her. I also tried to ignore her nudity, which wasn't easy. Angela was watching me, I noticed, and I wondered if this were some sort of game that she and Dawn were playing.

"Angie had been taking some shots of me," Dawn said, "then we suddenly noticed the time. We had to get to the supermarket before it closed. I just threw a coat over myself before we went out."

"I didn't know that," added Angela. "I thought she was dressing while I got the car out. When we reached the store, we got a trolley and started going around. I realised what Dawn was wearing when she reached up to one of the top shelves."

Dawn was pouring the tea. "Milk?" she asked me. "Sugar?"

"A little," I replied. "No thanks. And what was she wearing?" I asked, to show my interest in the story.

"The usual fantasy fashion underwear," said Angela, as she sipped at her own milkless, sugarless tea. "High heels, black stockings, suspenders, French knickers, transparent bra."

"But with a coat on top," said Dawn.

"An old coat, with most of the buttons missing."

Dawn shrugged, and her breasts bounced again.

"She reached up for something," Angela continued, "the top of the coat came loose, and I thought: what a great picture. So I took a couple of shots. A good photographer is never without her camera. Dawn saw what I was doing, so she opened her coat."

"I knew that was what you wanted. And it was, because you took more pictures."

"The more I took, the less you wore!" Angela looked at me. "There we were, in a supermarket full of people, and Dawn keeps taking her clothes off! First the coat, then the bra . . ."

"You didn't try to stop me, did you? You kept on photographing me, but it was me who had to do the shopping."

"There she was, peeling off what little she wore, choosing stuff from the shelves, and no one in the store took any notice!"

"Yes, they did! When my bra came off, some old fellow nearly fainted. After I dropped my panties, I was followed by a bunch of young guys."

"No one from the store, I mean." Angela took another sip of tea. "We were wandering around the supermarket, with Dawn down to her high heels. She was stretching up, bending down, posing as provocatively as she could. And nobody came up to ask what we were doing. The staff must have thought we had permission, I suppose, although none of the men in the place had any complaints. By the time we reached the checkout we had attracted quite an audience, which was hardly surprising. Dawn was sitting in the trolley by this time. Totally naked."

"That was your idea."

"Maybe. But you didn't have to empty everything all over yourself. What a waste! As for that banana . . . !"

They both laughed.

Angela put down her cup and stood up. She went to the bookshelves, and selected one of the ancient leather-bound volumes. Opening it up, she pulled out a glossy magazine. I recognised the type of publication. She flicked through the pages until she found what she wanted, then handed it to me.

"Take a look," she said.

It was the feature the two of them had been describing, a whole series of pictures in which Dawn did her shopping – meanwhile stripping off in the store. There were plenty of other people in the supermarket, and it did seem that none of them was paying any attention to her.

I'd seen plenty of photos of nudes recently, and they had all left me cold. This was what I expected, because such pictures weren't aimed at me; they were there for men to look at.

The photos of Dawn were far less explicit than most I had seen, yet somehow the juxtaposition of a naked girl in mundane surroundings was visually very exciting – even to me. Could this have anything to do with the fact that I was studying photos of a girl who was sitting opposite me? It couldn't be, I reasoned, because Dawn was as naked now as she was in her pictures. Maybe it was she who was having an effect on me. I kept my eyes down, studying the pictures instead.

The sequence had been printed as a comic strip, with captions next to the photos, and speech and thought bubbles coming from Dawn. These parts were Don's work. The title was *Charlotte's Shopping Spree*.

The first picture was of Dawn in her overcoat, pushing a trolley along one of the aisles. *Shopping always makes Charlotte hot and bothered*, said the caption. The next picture showed the front of her coat unfastened, revealing her scanty underwear.

A "thinks" bubble to the next picture read: 'I'm still too hot – but there's one way to cool off.' And "Charlotte" was shown shedding her coat.

The next few shots illustrated her selecting items from the shelves. Then she was unclipping the front of her bra, opening it to reveal her breasts, before discarding the garment. Then there was more shopping. Next she was thumbing down her French knickers, dropping them into the trolley and strolling through the store, buttocks bare. The stockings were next to go, first the left, then the right, and then the suspender belt. She kept her high heels on as she continued filling her trolley, pushing it along the aisles. Her boobs rose as she stretched up for an item on the top shelf; and her bum was high whenever she bent for something from the bottom shelf.

All the time there were captions and bubbles. 'I suppose it's my own fault for getting so hot. Shopping is so boring that I keep thinking of other things. Or one other thing! And that makes me even hotter. The hotter I get, the more I have to take off. And the more I have to take off, the hotter I get! But at least it makes shopping a pleasure instead of a chore.'

This was Don's wonderful prose, I realised. It was the first time I had read any of his commercial writing. (Although I might have unknowingly encountered some of it when I had been doing my researches.) It was only towards the end of the sequence that the writing began to rise above the prosaic. Perhaps Don was inspired by the pictures which showed Dawn lying back in the wire trolley, opening bottles and packets and jars, pouring the contents over her bare breasts and massaging them into her pubic hairs. She was covered with everything from flour and ketchup to cereal and marmalade.

'Sugar and spice and all things nice. We always knew Charlotte was good enough to eat, but here's the proof!' said the caption.

'I was sticky all over, both inside and out!' said the "thinks" bubble.

'With honey in my honey-pot, I wished my man was there to lick me clean!' said the next one, while the caption said: 'And the proof is always in the eating . . .'

'Instead I had to make do with what was to hand.' The penultimate picture showed Dawn peeling a banana. In the final one, she was holding it across her spread crotch. Her eyes were shut and her mouth was open as if in ecstasy. 'But a banana was just too soft to fill me up. What I needed was a good hard cock inside me. I couldn't wait until the shopping was over!'

I looked up from what I'd been reading and reached for my cup. Angela was now sitting next to Dawn.

"A good hard cock," said Angela. "Ha! That's the last thing Dawn needs."

Then she turned, put her arms around Dawn, and they kissed passionately.

My heart skipped a beat. This was another part of their game, I realised, some other test that Angela was putting me through to discover my reaction.

I saw Dawn watching me, even though she was still locked in an embrace with Angela, and she winked at me.

It was only then that I spilled my tea.

FIVE

All of the apparently old volumes on the shelves were in fact binders which held Angela's vast collection of magazines – those in which she had appeared, and those for which she had taken photographs. She showed some of them to me while we spoke, and everything she said was taped by my new digital recorder.

"I always wanted to be a model," she said, "but I suppose that's the ambition of many girls. There's modelling, however." She showed me a fashion magazine which had her face on the cover; she could only have been seventeen or eighteen at the time. "And there's modelling." She opened another magazine to the centre pages, which showed her lying naked on her back, her thighs wide apart, the lips of her vagina swollen and moist, her index finger caressing her clitoris.

"Things started well for me," she continued. "I was on the cover of several of the glossies, I did fashion features for all kinds of magazines, I flew all over the world for different shoots or to parade on catwalks. It was great for a while, I seemed to have the world at my feet. But then . . ." She shrugged.

"What happened?" I prompted.

"I wasn't tall enough, they said. I wasn't slender enough. My tits were too big. But the real reason was I wouldn't fuck the right people. A good-looking girl can fuck her way to the top in that kind of line, because what other talent does it take to be a fashion model? There's thousands of girls as good-looking as the top models, thousands better-looking. All they have to do is smile, either walk up and down, or stand still to be photographed – and suck off advertising directors."

"And you refused?"

"Not at first. I never liked it. But what was a mouthful of spunk compared to a week in Tahiti? After a while I wouldn't take that kind of treatment any more. I thought I'd got beyond it, that I didn't have to pay the price. I'd done a car advert, I was in magazines all over the world, so I thought I'd got it made. I was wrong, I wasn't big enough. Word got around, I suppose – Angela keeps her pants on and her mouth shut – and the work dried up. There were always plenty of other girls who would drop their knickers or open their mouths for the chance of a magazine cover."

She showed me the advertising feature for the car, in which she was standing by the vehicle in the middle of a desert. It must have been Australia, because there was a kangaroo in the picture.

"Any regrets?" I asked.

"The travelling was great. I liked flying and I even enjoyed jet-lag! I missed that at first. These days I can afford to pay for my own travelling, and I do foreign shoots whenever I can."

"Please," I said, as Dawn offered more tea. I glanced around the studio. "You do other kinds of photography?"

Angela shook her head. "Only glamour. Girls, girls, girls."

"But you go around the world?"

"I see what you mean." She gestured to the car advert again. "Was there any need for that to be taken in Australia? Not really. They wanted an exotic location, and it cost a fortune just to get the car there. It's the same with glamour photography. A girl on a bed could be anywhere. Paris, New

York, Moscow. But if you can take pictures of the girl which prove she really is in Paris, New York or Moscow, so much the better."

"You mean naked?"

"Not necessarily. Take a look at this." Angela found another binder, another magazine. She opened it and passed it to me.

The feature was titled "The Girls of Venice" and the first two pages showed three girls at various sites in the city, on the bridges, in gondolas. There were pictures of them singly and together, and they were fully dressed. In later pages they weren't, and the pictures were very restrained. The nudity seemed natural, without any convoluted positions. Even when all three girls were naked together, it seemed very innocent.

"It's nice to do something like this," said Angela. "The classier the magazine, the less explicit the pictures. That makes it harder for the photographer, because you aren't relying on the models so much. The eroticism has to come from your own inventiveness. Some of my best work has been done in black and white, I think. With black and white, you can't take the easy route and rely on pink."

"Pink?" I said.

Angela smiled. "You don't know?"

I shook my head.

"Show pink," she said to Dawn.

Dawn was still naked, and I'd almost grown used to her nudity. She set down her cup and saucer, leaned back in her chair, parted her thighs, slipped her fingers between her legs and pushed back the lips of her vagina.

My heartbeat was suddenly racing as I gazed at Dawn's cunt, and I couldn't tear my eyes away until she sat up again.

70

I knew that I was also showing pink, although of a different kind. I could feel myself blushing. As a redhead, I always blushed easily, but I hadn't gone as red as this for years – probably since I'd seen my first erection.

Seeing Dawn's twat was a very similar experience, I supposed, and hence the similar reaction.

"Don't be shy," said Angela, with another smile. "You've got one."

I almost said, *Yes, but I don't show mine to everyone.* If I had done, the interview would have abruptly ended; so would my planned articles for Jeff.

Instead, I also managed a smile. I tried to think of a way to change the subject.

"Have you got a lover?" asked Angela. "Or more than one?"

"What? Er – yes," I lied. "I live with him."

"Him? What a waste." Angela shook her head, then she noticed Dawn watching her and she laughed.

"She's only trying to make me jealous," said Dawn. "Only women are allowed up here, you know."

"I don't seduce all of them," said Angela.

"But you try!"

They both laughed, and I smiled nervously, hoping that it didn't look a nervous smile. When Angela had spoken about herself and Dawn having to go out to do the shopping, I knew they lived together. And when they had kissed, it was obvious that Dawn was no mere live-in employee.

"Angie could make a fortune if she was willing to photograph men," said Dawn, "but she refuses."

"Men?" I said.

"Yeah, those people with cocks."

"Photos of men, I mean."

71

"Not just men," said Dawn. "Men and women, you know."

"Ah," I said, although I didn't really know.

"Fuck 'em," said Angela. "But not literally."

Dawn caught my eye, and she winked again. This time I understood. The first time it had happened, Angela had been saying that a hard cock was the last thing Dawn needed. It seemed, however, that Dawn did not entirely agree.

I tried to remember what we had been talking about, but I kept thinking of how Dawn had revealed her cunt. It had been as casual as opening her mouth. For her, it probably was.

"You started as a fashion model," I said to Angela, "and now you're a photographer. In between? How did you get from one to the other?"

"As I told you," she said, "I gave up cock, which meant I no longer got any really good jobs. And I suppose the reason I gave up was because I realised I preferred women to men. I had to earn a living, and all I knew was modelling. The only difference was that it was me who was being photographed, not what I wore. I started with topless work, then went on to full nudity, then the more intimate stuff." She gestured to some of the magazines which were lying around.

"You never found it . . ." I paused, trying to choose the right words. ". . . difficult?"

"Say it. 'Degrading,' that's what you mean, isn't it?"

"No," I insisted, and I shook my head.

"It's a job. And it's a good job. It's a lot better than being a shop assistant or a receptionist. I know, because I tried both. I took my clothes off, but so what? It's part of a great artistic tradition. The nude has been the subject of statues and paintings throughout history. I only posed for photographs. I didn't do it in the street, flashing my twat at strangers."

"Yes you did," said Dawn.

"Well . . . not often! It was the same kind of thing as Dawn in the supermarket. Nudes indoors, on beaches, it had all been done thousands of times. But in public, that's different! The contrast can be quite effective. Let's see."

Angela stood up and hunted through her magazine collection again, producing various outdoor pictures of herself in the nude: sitting in a car at traffic lights, with the man in the car alongside staring in astonishment; gazing into a shop window; in a children's playground, on the swings, the slide, the roundabout; riding a bicycle along a busy street.

"They were my idea," she said. "But I never made much money from them, or from any of my pictures. It was the photographer who earned it all, and it took me a long time to realise that. There are always far more girls than photographers."

"So you decided to become one?" I said.

"She had no alternative," said Dawn. "She was getting too old, her tits sagging, her bum drooping, her teeth falling out . . . Hey!" She threw up her arm defensively, ducking to avoid the magazine which Angela hurled at her.

"Dawn will soon be in a similar situation to me," said Angela. "No one will want to use her any more because she's been seen in too many magazines too many times."

"Over-exposed," said Dawn. "Although you should never use that word to a photographer; it's an insult."

"I was in magazines all over the world," Angela continued, "under so many different names, with so many different wigs and hairstyles. From topless through to . . . well, anything that didn't involve men."

"But they were male photographers?" I said

73

"All but one. They could look, but they couldn't touch – just the same as anyone seeing my picture in a magazine."

"And the other one? That was a woman?"

"Miranda, yes. She was an ex-model. She took the most superb pictures, the horniest stuff I've ever been in. Miranda was straight, alas, but she had a real feel for two girl sets. She was turned on by what she was doing, but she never got involved with any of her models. Not even the men. She was a true professional."

Angela produced another magazine, it was a foreign one, and I felt myself starting to blush again as I looked at the first photos of Angela and a slim brunette and what they were doing to each other. I'd read about women behaving this way with each other; lesbianism was one of the favourite subjects in the men's magazines. In the past I'd even had similar fantasies involving myself and other girls, but I'd never imagined that photographs of such intimate involvement were published.

My whole body was damp with sweat. I tried to blame the summer heat, but that wouldn't explain the way my pulse had increased. But I was particularly hot and damp between my legs, and I knew I couldn't blame the climate for that.

Angela and her companion were both nude, except for black leather: knee-length boots, studded belts around their waists, matching straps around their necks and chokers around their throats. I stared at the pictures where they kissed, their tongues thrust out and pressed together. Then they stroked one another's breasts, licking the erect nipples. Their hands moved lower, and they began fingering each other's cunts. Fingers rubbed against swollen clits, before slipping deep inside moist twats. Then they switched positions so that tongues could replace hands, their fingers gliding against swollen pink labia, then sliding within.

"May I use the bathroom?" I asked, standing up.

"Through the door and second on the left," Angela told me.

"Feeling randy, huh?" asked Dawn. "Want to bring yourself off? Don't mind us. If fact, we can help . . ."

I wasn't sure what I did want. Dawn was partly correct, because I felt very aroused. An orgasm would relieve the tension, and I could tell it wouldn't take me long to climax. But I could also do with a cold shower. That was impossible, so I would have to be content with a drink of water.

I locked the bathroom door and gazed at myself in the mirror, then ran the cold tap and splashed my face with water. It was hard to believe that the photographs had had such an affect on me. A girl licking another's cunt, that's all it was. As I thought about it, I couldn't help wonder what it would be like to have a girl perform cunnilingus on me – and what it was like to do it . . .

There was a heavy knock on the door. "I know what you're doing in there!" shouted Dawn, and she laughed. "Want to borrow my vibrator?"

I drank some water before opening the door.

"Hot, isn't it?" I said, wiping my face with a tissue.

"Not for me," said Dawn.

"You always walk around like that?"

She glanced down at her nude body. "Whenever I can." She gestured towards the studio. "First time you've seen that kind of thing?" she asked, referring to the pictures of Angela and the other girl.

"No, of course not." I shook my head, then thought of

something else. "When you talked about Angela not having men up here, you meant . . . ?"

"Yeah." Dawn nodded.

"Photos of actual fucking?"

"Actual fucking with actual men, actual sucking, actual everything. One guy, one girl. Two guys, one girl. One guy, two girls. Three guys, two girls, one giraffe! You want to see some?"

I shook my head again. I'd seen more than enough for one day.

"Don't let Angie know I've still got any. But she keeps all her stuff, so I don't see why I can't keep mine. Maybe some other time?"

"Maybe," I said.

In a way I wanted to leave, but I remembered how several days ago I'd walked out of the Italian restaurant because I couldn't handle the way things were going. Now I had to stay in order to continue the interview. And I also wanted to stay, I realised, fascinated by what I had already discovered. Whatever was to come, I was sure I could take it.

"Maybe," I repeated. "I can interview you later, can I?"

"Yeah."

"So," I said to Angela, as we resumed, "having worked with Miranda, you decided to become a photographer?"

"Not immediately, although I knew I couldn't keep on as a model forever. But that was the world I knew, moving to the other side of the camera was a logical progression. That was where the money way, and I had to think of my future. There was no chance of me marrying, of some man supporting me." She paused as if contemplating the prospect.

"Miranda took you on as an assistant?"

"No chance!" said Angela. "She didn't want any competition. I had to work for men in order to learn, but it wasn't the same as when I started out modelling. I didn't have to fuck my way into a job. I was lucky, I found a guy who preferred his own sex. Because I preferred my own, it was a perfect arrangement."

"He wasn't worried that you'd become a competitor?"

"George didn't take me seriously at first. I'd modelled for him many times, and when I started asking about cameras and lenses and apertures, all he said was, 'The only aperture you have to concern yourself with, sweetie, is that of your cunt.' But I suppose it was nice for him to work with a girl who took such an interest in the job. He had a big argument with his assistant one day when I was there, and he took me on. I owe George a lot. He'd learned from another photographer, and now Dawn is learning from me."

"What advantages does a female photographer have over a male?"

"Everything!" Angela laughed. She glanced over towards her apartment, where Dawn still was. "Or at least I do."

"Go on."

"The whole idea of glamour photography is to take sexy pictures, pictures which will turn on the guys who look at them. The only way to do that really well is if the photographer is excited by what is happening. And I get *really* turned on, just as a male photographer would."

"What about George?"

"That was kind of different. Knowing his inclinations, all the girls tried extra hard to turn him on when they were posing. They always make love to the camera, in a sense. And George was regarded as a challenge. He knew this and he played on it, which is why he was so good at photographing

77

girls. He likes to pretend it's no different from doing land-scapes, but I know how much he enjoys it."

"You get turned on by the girls, but how do they react to you?"

"I like to think they're less inhibited with me, more likely to give that little bit extra. Some of them prefer male photo-graphers, because they like to fantasise they're fucking them – and, of course, it often ends up as more than a fantasy. But most of them can relax more with a woman, I think. We have things in common. We can talk together, laugh together." She shrugged, glancing towards the door again. "And sometimes do other things together."

"Yes," I said, aware of the pictures of her and the brunette which were still on the table in front of us.

"If what I'm doing gets me horny," said Angela, "then it must do the same for men. What are all these pictures about? What is it that I photograph?"

"Girls. Nude girls."

"But which part? What is the focus of almost every shot?"

"You mean . . . ?"

"It's cunt, right? That's what men want to see, that's what I give them. And they say we have penis envy? Ha! Cunt envy, that's what they've got."

"Penis envy, huh?" said Dawn, as she came back into the studio. "You know what they say: if you've got a cunt, you can get a cock any time!" She noticed Angela watching her. "A joke," she said. "Just a joke."

Angela glanced up at the grandfather clock next to her. I switched off the recorder and stood up.

"No, no," said Angela, as she also stood up, "that wasn't a hint. It seems the new model isn't going to turn up. I might as well do something with Dawn." She walked over to the girl and stroked her left breast. "You want to watch?"

"What?" I said.

"My turn to joke," she said. "I'll shoot off a few rolls of film and you can see how it's done. Yes?"

"Yes," I said.

"You don't mind an audience, Dawn, do you?"

"Of course not, and she's already seen everything."

"Good." Angela walked deeper into the studio.

"Have you, er, known each other long?" I asked.

Dawn nodded, and she stepped towards the mirrored corner. There was a wooden rail along one of the walls. I only recognised its purpose when Dawn put her right hand on the bar to steady herself, then raised her right leg and rested it along the rail. It was as if she were in a dance studio.

"We first met when Angie was still modelling," she said, raising her arms in the air. In the mirror, her nude reflection did the same, her breasts rising. "We did two girl stuff, simulated tongue-fucking, our tongues not quite touching our twats. If only I'd known what I was missing! Angie can give better head than anyone else I know, male or female." She sighed at the thought. "Anyhow, it's a small world, our paths kept crossing. She became a photographer, and occasionally I was her model. I was touching myself up for her camera one day, and she was showing me where to put my fingers. Next thing I knew it was her fingers that were touching me up, and there was no simulation this time. We didn't get much work done that day."

As she spoke, Angela kept on stretching her limbs, like a nude ballet dancer going through her exercises. She extended her right leg along the bar, facing the mirror as she did so. I saw a glint of pink. Then the right leg went down, the left leg came up, and again the mirror caught the reflection of her cunt.

"Sometimes the contortions you have to go into for a picture are ridiculous," said Dawn. "The kind of poses no girl ever gets into, all just so the camera can see your twat from a different angle. You have to be almost double-jointed. Angie always tries to make it look natural." She thrust her pubis towards the mirror, and her inner labia parted even more, revealing even more pink.

I glanced up and met Dawn's eyes in the mirror. She smiled, knowing where my gaze had been a moment earlier. She twisted around and off the bar, went up on her toes, pirouetted, then suddenly did the splits. Her legs seemed impossibly far apart, and her cunt seemed as wide as it could possibly be.

"Like that," she said, gazing down at herself.

I had my doubts about the naturalness of the pose; most ballet dancers tended to wear costumes.

"Over here!" called Angela from the far side of the studio, and we went to join her.

I walked slightly behind Dawn, as if following her, but really so that I could admire her supple body. I envied her sleek poise, the way she was so relaxed about her own sexuality. But people were different, and I was different. I had always been shy and reserved; there was no way I could alter my personality.

"What are the orders today, boss?" she asked, saluting.

Angela was switching on huge lamps, which were focused on a tiger-skin that lay over a bed. On the wall above the bed were various stuffed animal heads, all of them with horns or antlers.

"Fake fur," Dawn told me, stroking the striped skin.

"We're both vegetarian. In fact the only meat that ever enters my mouth . . ." She let the sentence trail away as Angela glared at her.

"Let's use a rifle as the main prop," said Angela.

"Subtle phallic suggestion, huh?" said Dawn. "I'll get the stuff." She went back the way we had come.

"Anything I can do?" I asked.

"Can you load a camera?"

"Only an automatic."

Angela shook her head and moved a tripod nearer the bed. Dawn returned a minute or two later, clutching a handful of items. She began doing her make-up, laying on the lipstick and eyeshadow and lashes very heavily. She ran a brush through her dark hair.

"Now for the real tricks of the trade," she said, as she used the brush on her pubic hairs. Then she aimed a canister of hairspray at her pubis. "Ozone-friendly," she explained, pressing the button.

She had also brought a glass in which ice-cubes floated, and had been sipping at the drink while doing her face. Now she reached into the glass and lifted out two of the cubes, which she rubbed against her nipples. It only took a few seconds before they became fully erect, standing out from the dark pink of the areolae.

"There's less of a tit problem in winter," said Dawn, as she dropped one of the cubes back into her drink and pushed the other into her mouth. "Now for the final touch of verisimilitude." She reached for the last item she had brought. It was a bottle of baby oil and she poured some into her left hand, dipped the fingers of her right into the pool, then . . .

I watched in astonishment as she opened her legs and began rubbing the oil against the lining of her vagina.

"Wet and eager," she said, and she stroked her fingertip against her clitoris – which visibly dilated as she did so.

I had passed beyond the blushing stage by now, and my own throbbing vagina felt as slick and swollen as Dawn's.

"Stop playing with yourself!" Angela ordered, with mock severity.

"Just making sure it's well rubbed in," protested Dawn, but she reluctantly withdrew her fingers from her twat.

"On the bed," said Angela.

"I thought we were working," said Dawn, with a laugh.

"We are!" insisted Angela, suddenly becoming serious. She now had a camera around her neck, and it was as if she had become a different person.

Dawn glanced at me, shrugged, then hurled herself down onto the tiger skin. She lay on her back and raised her legs, spreading them wide as she gripped her ankles with her hands, and her cunt was more exposed than ever, pink and glistening, the inner labia drawn back.

"That isn't what I want," said Angela, "and you know it." Even so, she took a few quick pictures as she spoke.

Dawn let her legs drop, sat up and reached over for the props by the bed. She slung two bandoliers across her shoulders. They hung to her waist, criss-crossing her breasts. She drew on a pair of knee-length stockings; they were striped in yellow and black, making her legs seem even longer. A camouflaged military cap completed her outfit. She picked up the rifle, resting the stock against her crotch and holding it up at an angle.

Angela began photographing her, shouting out commands and encouragement. Dawn didn't need many orders, she knew what was wanted of her. She used the rifle as a substitute penis, kissing the barrel, running her tongue along its length, rubbing it across her nipples, stroking it against her twat, sliding herself along the cold metal. It was as if she were fucking the weapon. Her eyes were closed, her mouth open. She squirmed on her back, rolled over on all fours, caressed and stroked the long shaft, did everything except slide it inside herself.

As I watched, my heart pounded and I felt the blood pulse throughout my body. Every inch of my flesh was speckled with sweat. I ached to the core of my being for release.

"Right, that's it," said Angela.

Her collection of cameras had run out of film, and Dawn let herself drop back on the bed. She was also damp with sweat, I noticed. Her breasts rose and fell with her heartbeat. But she had no problem with release, because her right hand lay across her crotch, two fingers buried deep within. Her hips rocked up and down as she calmly masturbated herself. And I saw that she was gazing at me, as if it were me who was exciting her. I managed to tear my own eyes away. It really was time to leave.

"Try this," said Angela, beckoning to me. By now she had reloaded one of her camera. "Stop that," she said to Dawn, noticing what she was doing. Dawn stuck out her tongue and kept on fingering herself.

I went over to Angela, who handed me the camera.

"You should see what it's like through a viewfinder," she said. "Turn the outer ring to focus."

I looked through the camera, but it was Angela who I looked at. I tried to forget Dawn and what she was doing.

"I'm not used to this," Angela laughed, and she peeled off her running vest, baring her breasts. "By your right finger, that's the shutter control. Just press."

I took her photograph.

"And another. It's automatic." She cupped her breasts and pouted.

I obeyed, taking another picture.

Angela slipped out of her shorts, and she was as naked as all the pictures I had seen of her. Her pubic curls were as pale as her hair, her body still as fit and lithe and sensual and erotic as when she had been modelling.

I felt oddly detached from what I was seeing, as if the viewfinder distanced me from Angela's naked body. She had stripped off her clothes not for me, it seemed, but for the camera. But as well as separating me from Angela, the camera also brought me closer — as I discovered when I turned the lens, bringing her nude body even nearer.

She went through a series of exaggerated poses, sticking out her boobs, or jutting out one hip, or turning and thrusting her buttocks towards me, glancing back over her shoulder and blowing a kiss. It was all far more innocent than the manoeuvring which Dawn had gone through as she writhed on the bed.

At any moment, I sensed, Angela would probably join Dawn. While I held her transfixed in the viewfinder, however, it appeared as if she were under my control.

And then the shutter would press down no more, the whole film had been used up.

"That was fun," said Angela. "Thanks."

She came towards me, and I handed the camera to her. I glanced at Dawn, who was now sitting up on the bed, then back to Angela. They were both naked, and they were both staring at me.

"We've talked," said Angela. "You've seen a session. You've used a camera. There's only one thing left, isn't there?"

I nodded.

There was only one way to find out what it was really like to be a nude model.

SIX

The first naked male I ever saw was James. He was about a year older than me, still a teenager, too old to be a boy, too young to be a man.

I was staying with Rebecca for the weekend, and James was her brother. Their parents lived in a huge house in the country, complete with its own stables and two huge swimming pools – one indoors, one outdoors.

I'd gone ahead to the indoor pool, and Rebecca was to meet me there in a few minutes. The swimming pool was amazing, because it was completely landscaped to look like a tropical lake. It was surrounded by exotic plants and palm trees, fed by a waterfall which cascaded across the rocks at one end. As I walked around the pool, I didn't notice James. We saw each other at the same time. It was the first time we had met.

"Oh," he said, as surprised as I was, "hello."

"Hello," I said. "I'm a friend of Rebecca's."

"I'm not," he replied, pulling a face. "I'm her brother."

It was obvious he'd been swimming. His hair was wet, his body was damp, and he was holding a towel around his waist.

"How's the water?" I asked.

"Great. It's always great."

"Where's the changing room?"

"There isn't one," he said. He gestured to his clothes which lay on a nearby wicker chair. "You have to undress here."

"But I have to put my swimsuit on."

"You don't need one," said James. "We never wear them."

As he spoke he removed the towel from his waist and began to dry his back. He wasn't wearing a costume.

I stared at him, or rather at one part of him. I was both astonished and embarrassed, and I felt myself begin to blush as I gazed at his cock, but I was unable to look away.

I'd never seen one before, not in the flesh.

I didn't have a brother, and the only penises I'd ever seen had been those of baby boys. Like all other girls, I'd wondered what the male of the species kept inside their pants. I'd studied biology texts, I'd looked at classical statues, I'd even seen photos of naked men. But none of this prepared me for what James had on display.

Fascinated and yet horrified, I gazed at his full-grown prick. And as I did so, it began to grow even more . . .

James stood two yards away from me, totally naked, his penis becoming more swollen as it rose towards the vertical. This was the first adult penis I had ever seen, and also the first hard-on. I felt myself grow even redder. I knew all about the theory of human reproduction, but to see half of the necessary equipment so blatantly displayed was both shocking and exciting.

"Get your clothes off," said James. "What's the point of wearing something in the water? It will only get wet. You don't wear anything in the bath, do you?"

I didn't know what to say, what to do, how to react. Meanwhile, James's prick was fully erect, swaying slightly from side to side as he dried himself. I was aware that his knob had become erect because of me, which gave me a very strange feeling.

Then suddenly James wrapped his towel around his waist. I looked around and noticed the door to the house was open. Rebecca came through and walked towards us.

"I see you've met my brother," she said. "I think he must have been adopted. He's too ugly to be my real brother."

I wasn't too sure of that; James was very good-looking.

"And too clever," said James.

"Let's get changed," said Rebecca, and she walked past her brother, making as wide a detour as was possible.

I followed, and there was a changing room. We got undressed together, although we kept our backs to one another. When I saw Rebecca, I felt overdressed. She was wearing the most abbreviated of fluorescent bikinis. Her ripe breasts were barely covered by the bra, and the pants hardly covered her pubis. My one-piece costume seemed very Victorian.

There was no sign of James when we entered the pool. But he had been correct: the water was great. The temperature was exactly right, and I could have stayed in there for hours. We swam up and down, we played and splashed water at each other, we tried to drag each other below the surface, we floated and we talked, and finally Rebecca suggested we go into the hot tub.

"What's that?" I asked.

"Never tried one? It's wonderful. You'll love it! Come on."

We climbed from the main pool and walked to a much smaller one, from which steam was rising. Rebecca pressed a switch on the wall, and the water within the huge bath began to foam and bubble. I followed her down the ladder. The water was far hotter, and there was was ledge on which we could sit, with just our heads above the surface.

Powerful streams of water jetted against my back from the

wall behind me. It was like being massaged, and was both relaxing and invigorating at the same time.

"Great, huh?" said Rebecca, and I could see that her whole body was vibrating in the foaming water. "Must get comfortable." She turned around to face the side of the pool, kneeling on the ledge, and she pressed herself hard against the wall.

I wasn't sure what she was doing at first, until I realised her crotch must have been directly opposite one of the water jets. Even then I wasn't too certain what she was up to. But whatever Rebecca was doing, she was enjoying herself.

Her eyes were closed, her lips slightly parted. One of her hands was on the lip of the pool, but her other hand was out of sight, stroking each breast in turn. Although beneath the swirling water, I could see as her fingers slid within the fabric of her bikini top, caressing her flesh. I glimpsed each of her nipples as she circled them between her fingertips. Then her hand vanished, sinking deeper into the water. I tried not to look; but as with James, I couldn't look away. Rebecca was oblivious to me, however, to anything and everything apart from her obvious pleasure.

She gasped and sighed, moaned and panted, then finally drifted into the centre of the tub and sank beneath the surface of the bubbling pool. At last she reappeared, smiling contentedly.

"I needed that," she muttered, finally opening her eyes.

I nodded, as though I understood what she meant.

"I'll leave you to it, shall I?" she asked.

I nodded again, and she climbed the ladder, tugging up her bikini pants as she did so. They had slipped down in the churning waters.

Rebecca could do this whenever she wanted, it was no

novelty for her. But I wanted to spend as long as I could in the luxurious water, and I also wanted to be alone – to discover exactly what it was that was so pleasurable. I could guess, but I wanted to find out for myself.

I was still so innocent. I'd never had a boyfriend, never even been kissed. All the other girls I knew boasted about what they had done, from having a tongue down their throats to a hand inside their panties – and more. But to me all of this was unknown. All I knew was what I had read about, and I spent the majority of my time reading. I wanted to be a writer, so reading was part of my training.

When Rebecca had gone into the changing room, I also turned around and pressed my crotch against one of the water vents, letting the pressure pound against my pubis. The force was very strong and took some getting used to. I wasn't in the habit of giving that part of my body such attention.

As well as studying male anatomy, I'd also checked out the reference books on female genitalia. None of it had made much sense to me. I'd never been able to work out which bit was which and had begun to believe that my own private parts were abnormal. Even examining myself in a mirror hadn't done any good; I'd become more con-fused than ever, convinced there was something wrong with me.

As well as studying the classics of literature, I often read contemporary novels, the kind of blockbusters written by women; books filled with exotic sex and expensive lifestyles. These had comprised the sum total of my sex education, and I didn't believe most of them.

It was like the first time I ever heard about reproduction. Animals, okay. That was just instinct. But when we moved on

90

up to humans? I couldn't believe that. A man puts his *what* inside a woman's *what* . . . ? You've got to be kidding!

I'd finally accepted that the facts of human mating were true, but I still had difficulty with novels where the sex was more than basic. A man puts his *what* inside a woman's mouth! A man puts his tongue inside a woman's *what* . . . !

I felt guilty about what I was doing in the whirlpool, although that was beginning to fade as I started to enjoy myself. But then the timer switched itself off, the water ceased to bubble, and it was as if I was simply in a hot bath. I noticed Rebecca leaving the changing room, dressed in shorts and T-shirt.

"Shall I switch it on again?" she asked, grinning.

"That's okay," I said, quickly. "I'm coming out now."

"Don't be long," she said. "I'll order some tea."

Order some tea. She made it sound as if we were in a restaurant instead of her home.

I climbed out of the whirlpool and went into the changing room, locking the door behind me. There was a shower inside, and I peeled off my swimsuit, allowing the cool spray to splash all over my body. I spent a long time in the shower, much longer than usual, allowing my hands to linger on my breasts, feeling the hardness of my swollen nipples against my palms. Then my hands moved lower, towards the forbidden area where they had seldom lingered before, remembering the pressure of the water forcing itself against my crotch. My fingers roved between my pubic hairs, moving further and deeper, then quickly withdrawing.

I had thought I was alone, yet now it seemed as though I was being watched. I glanced around, but the door was firmly shut, there were no windows. Switching off the shower, I quickly dried and dressed myself. Then I returned to the house, where the tea was waiting to be poured. Rebecca managed to do that herself.

After a few minutes, James came into the room. He was dressed in an expensive tracksuit, and his hair was still damp. He and Rebecca exchanged glances, but they said nothing. James looked at me.

"Nice to have seen you," he said, smiling.

And then I realised he meant that literally: he must have been watching when I was in the shower. I suddenly felt as naked as I had been in the changing room. James simply winked, then left the room. I glanced at Rebecca. She shrugged, knowing exactly what James had meant, then she smiled mischievously.

"He spies on my guests," she said. "And I spy on his. Do you mind?"

I wondered if Rebecca ever minded being spied upon, whether that was part of the arrangement she had with her brother. But there had been no need for me to spy upon James; he had been only too willing to expose himself.

Did I mind?

"No," I replied. "Why should I mind?" Even as I spoke, I knew it was the truth.

That was the way it had been ever since. I had never minded if a man saw me naked. But for another woman to see me nude . . . that was different.

The next day I returned to the swimming pool at the same time. Perhaps I was hoping James would repeat his performance for me. The previous night my dreams had been filled with strange images. I'd dreamed that I was lost in a jungle, that there were slithering snakes all around me, and I'd woken up hot and sweating.

James was there, but he was still in the pool. He was, however, naked. He rolled onto his back as soon as he saw me. I pretended to ignore him, even though he backstroked along the edge of the pool where I was walking. Because of the water, I couldn't tell if his cock was floating up from his crotch or whether it was vertical because it had grown hard.

"Not using the changing room today, are you?" he asked. "You're too late. You might as well come in naked. I've already seen you."

I ignored him, but I couldn't help wondering if he was going to climb from the pool. I wasn't sure whether I wanted him to or not, if I wanted to see him again, to see his prick stiffen and rise.

"You polluting that water?" called Rebecca.

James immediately rolled over on his front.

"We've got to swim in there, you know!" Rebecca added, striding along the side of the pool. "You be out of there in one minute, or else!"

James thrust his naked buttocks into the air, then dived beneath the surface. Rebecca and I went into the changing room, put on our swimsuits. By the time we emerged, James was out of the pool. There was a towel around his waist, and he watched as we dived into the water.

We swam, just like yesterday, then entered the hot tub. By this time there was no sign of James. And just like yesterday, Rebecca pressed herself up against one of the pulsing jets of water. I couldn't bring myself to do the same while she was still in the whirlpool with me. Like her brother, she seemed to have few inhibitions; but at least she didn't peel off her scanty suit while I was with her. Rebecca stroked and rubbed her breasts, then her hand moved down lower. Her whole body writhed, and her mouth was wide open in

93

ecstasy as she slowly sank beneath the surface. Her head emerged a few seconds later, and she squirted a stream of water from her lips. She sighed, then smiled.

"I'll see you later," she said, and she climbed out of the tub, again pulling her bikini pants up until they were tight between the glistening cheeks of her backside. "The tea will be ready when you are."

I watched as she headed towards the changing room. She unfastened her bikini top as she walked, slinging it over her shoulder. Meanwhile, beneath the swirling surface of the hot tub, I slipped my hands inside my swimsuit, feeling the hardness of my nipples against my palms. Then I turned, pressing my crotch up against one of the throbbing jets of water. The pulsing liquid cascaded against me, sending thrilling shudders up and down my body. It was almost as if I were being touched by someone else . . .

The water fountained against me, and I kept covering my crotch with my palm, waiting for a few seconds to pass before allowing the full force to pound against me again. But it wasn't the full force, I realised. My costume was deflecting much of the pressure – and the pleasure.

And so I tugged the edge of the fabric aside, allowing the stream to hit my exposed vagina, swirling over my public hairs, rippling through my labia and cascading across my clitoris. The sensation was wonderful. My cunt lips felt more swollen than ever before, and for the first time ever I was able to clutch my engorged clit between my fingertips. I was in paradise, my fingers and the warm water caressing the heart of my inner being, feeling a strange glow building up deep inside, a fire within myself which the waters could not quench – but which perhaps my probing fingers could.

I had touched and stroked myself before, but more out of

curiosity than from desire. Never had there been such immediacy, such realisation of impending achievement. I rubbed myself with more urgency, thrusting my hips up against the side of the tub, allowing the tidal wave to flow across my cunt.

Then, just like yesterday, the throbbing jets were abruptly cut off. I immediately drew my hand away and covered my exposed vagina, glancing around to ensure no one was watching what I had been doing. Waiting until I had regained my breath and my pulse had returned to normal, I climbed from the tub and headed for the changing room. I didn't go inside immediately, but checked the sides to make sure James wasn't hanging around to spy in me again. That was when I found the spyhole. I glanced through, and I could see inside very clearly. Then I went into the room, locked the door, peeled off my costume, then switched on the shower.

Even as I did so, I knew that James could not have been far away.

I turned the shower as hot as I could bear, filling the room with steam. I ran my soapy hands over my body, as if washing myself, but really I was continuing what I had begun in the hot tub. My palms stroked my breasts, then slid down over my ribcage, before moving around and over my hips, then across my buttocks. My left hand returned to my breasts, caressing each in turn, as finally I allowed my right hands to return to my crotch, sliding the soap across my pubic hairs.

My eyes were closed, my head tilted back as the hot spray jetted across my nude body, as the fingers of my right hand worked lower, deeper.

I was being watched, I realised. And I also realised that I didn't mind. Not only didn't I mind, but I enjoyed being spied upon.

James must have been gazing through the spyhole, and I

was giving him something worth watching. I became aware I was doing this for him, not for myself. Although I was fondling my boobs, caressing my cunt, I was doing it without any real passion; I was acting out a role.

The room was so filled with steam that James would only have been able to catch a few brief glimpses of what I was doing. An idea occurred to me, and slowly I backed towards the exit. Then I quickly turned, unlocked the door, pulled it open and hurried out.

I was naked, covered in soap.

James was naked, masturbating.

He didn't notice me at first, he was still peering through the hole in the wall. His vertical cock was in his right hand, his palm sliding around it, up and down, tugging the foreskin back and forth over the swollen glans.

Then he either realised that he could no longer see me, or else – as I had done a few minutes ago – he suddenly became aware that he was under observation.

My hands were on my hips, my legs astride. Water dripped from my nude body.

James looked around quickly. His hand became still. It was his turn to blush. He tried to cover himself with both hands. His face became as pink as his swollen tool. He opened his mouth to speak, but he said nothing.

"Don't let me interrupt," I said.

He took his hands away, exposing himself to me again. Then he wrapped his right hand around the base of his knob, and he cupped his balls in his left palm. His eyes were focused on me as he began to slide his right hand up and down, slowly at first.

I didn't move. I met James's eyes, then gazed down at his cock. I felt my pulse begin to increase, my nipples to dilate even more, and my crotch became as moist as it had been in the hot tub.

James kept wanking as I watched, but I kept my hands firmly on my hips, resisting the urge to touch myself. His eyes surveyed my body, finally aiming at my crotch, at the wet ginger hairs, at what he might have been able to see within. His hand moved faster and faster, up and down, up and down.

Then he suddenly grunted and his cock erupted, the first gush of spunk spurting upwards and then splashing onto the ground between us. But before it hit the tiles, another creamy squirt arced from the domed head of his penis. Then another, and another. And another.

I watched in awe as he offered me his virile libation.

Then there was no more, the show was over, and I returned to rinse the soap from my naked body.

I had to leave early the next morning, so there wouldn't be time for another swim – or to see James's cock again.

It had been an interesting weekend, I thought, as I lay in bed that final evening. Educational, too, because I'd learned more about male physiology in two days than I had done during the rest of my life. I knew the theory of erection, of course, how the male organ became engorged with blood which caused it to expand and become perpendicular. The theory, however, had never prepared me for the practice. Perhaps there was more to life than could be discovered in books. I'd seen nothing I hadn't read about, but there was a great difference between reading about a penis ejaculating and actually witnessing such a spectacular event.

And it was still an odd feeling to realise that had happened because of me. To watch as a limp length of flesh became swollen and stood to attention in my honour had been very strange. It made me realise for the first time the power of a female over a man, of my power over a man, of my innate sexuality.

I could understand James getting a hard-on the second time, when he had been a voyeur watching me caress my naked body in the shower. But the previous day his erection had occurred when I was fully dressed. The only stimulus he had needed was *me*, he wasn't merely turned on by my nudity.

This response had not been a one-way process, because I had also been excited. But it wasn't James himself, whether clad or unclad, who had been the focus of my attention. It had been his prick. That was the part of him which had fascinated me, but only when it had become aroused.

In its normal state, a cock was of absolutely no interest to any girl. It was ugly, without function. But once erect, it was transformed into something else. As a phallus it possessed its own potent splendour, and it also had a purpose: it was there to fuck.

But boy needed girl, man needed woman, cock needed cunt.

And that weekend, for the first time, I had become aware of my own latent sexuality. I had finally discovered the buried treasure which lay at the junction of my thighs.

Lying in bed, I was lazily fingering myself, enjoying the new sensation as I remembered James's knob and how it had spurted. I'd never imagined ejaculation would be like that, that it would happen so often, on and on, that so much sperm would be produced.

Then the door opened, and James stood there.

I was naked, and I pulled the covers up defensively.

"Can I come in?" he asked.

"No."

"You don't mean that." He entered the room, closing the door behind him. The only thing he wore was a pair of shorts, and I could see he already had a hard-on.

My left hand was holding the covers, but my right was still resting on my twat, my fingers lying over my labia. James glanced down, and it was as if he could see exactly what I was doing. He smiled.

"Can I watch?" he asked.

"Watch what?"

"I've never seen a girl frigging herself. You saw me, now it's my turn to see you. Yes?"

"Get out or I'll scream."

"No you won't. What do you think is going to happen? Don't be scared. I'm not going to touch you." He was still smiling. "But do you want to touch me?"

"No."

"Are you sure? You seemed so interested in watching me jerk off, I thought you might want to lend me a hand."

"You thought wrong."

James shrugged. "You haven't answered me yet."

"Answered what?"

"Can I watch you?" He nodded towards the lump in the bed, where my hand was poised over my cunt.

"Fuck off," I told him.

"What? Again? Okay, if you insist." He pushed down his pants and leaned back against the door, naked. His cock was almost rigid, reaching up towards his navel.

I gazed at his length of firm male flesh, from the purple tip down to the nest of black hair and the testicles which hung loosely beneath.

"You want a repeat performance?" he asked, as he ran his fingertips along the length of his tool.

It was my turn to shrug. "Do what you want."

"Remind me what you look like. I need some inspiration."

I'd let James see me nude in the shower earlier that day because I could pretend I didn't know he was watching. But the idea of revealing myself to him now was very tempting, because it seemed so daring and forbidden.

I let the covers fall away, baring my breasts, and my nipples grew even harder.

James's smile returned. "I wish Rebecca had more friends like you."

"You usually visit their rooms like this?"

"No. But when I realised that you were so interested in me . . ."

"I'm not," I told him. "I'm only interested in your prick." It was my turn to smile. "Are you going to start or just stand there?"

James started, curling his right hand into a fist and stroking it up and down the length of his cock. After a few strokes, he spat into his hand and rubbed his saliva around the domed head of his knob.

"Lubrication," he explained. "Just like pussy juice."

Beneath the covers, I rubbed my fingers together, feeling the real thing.

"You do this often?" I asked.

"Whenever I can."

"You?" he asked, his eyes gazing towards my crotch.

We could almost have been discussing how often we washed our hair.

"All the time," I said. By now my fingers were between my legs, gently caressing my labia, waiting for my clitoris to

100

respond. I made no attempt to hide what I was doing, deliberately moving the covers more than I needed to. My hand was working in rhythm with James's; we stroked ourselves at the same pace.

"What kind of fantasies do you have?"

I said nothing, because I had no answer.

"Do you pretend you're being fucked, being sucked?" asked James, as his hand began to move slightly faster. "Sometimes I imagine that, pretending I'm sliding my dick into a tight twat or a hot mouth. Other times I flick through nude magazines, just looking at the pictures while I wank. But today's the only time I've had an audience." He stared at me, but I remained silent.

"It seems such a waste," he continued, "you using your hand, me using mine. Wouldn't it be much better if we did it to one another?"

I shook my head, but my eyes continued gazing at his knob, watching as his balls tightened.

"At least let me see what you're doing," he said.

Slowly I pushed the covers further down, then kicked them away from my legs. The bedclothes hung almost off me; one of my hips was bare; I held the covers across my crotch with my left hand, while the fingers of my right continued teasing my budding clit.

James was breathing faster now, his hand moving up and down more swiftly. My own breath matched his, although my fingertips weren't stroking myself quite so frantically.

Then I let the covers fall away. I lay there naked, playing with my cunt.

"Fuck!" gasped James, as he came.

He gripped his spurting prick tightly, and white streamers jetted even further than before. He stepped closer, aiming his knob towards me – and a ribbon of hot spunk splattered across my stomach and chest.

I rubbed my fingers in the stuff, feeling its strange texture, then massaged it into my flesh, across my breasts and nipples. My hips jerked involuntarily, and I closed my eyes in total ecstasy as I achieved my first-ever orgasm. My whole body glowed with a radiant warmth which flowed out from the centre of my contented cunt.

When I finally opened my eyes, James was looking a little guilty, probably for spunking over me. But guilt was the last thing that I felt, and I smiled at him.

"Do it again," I said. "I'd like to see a replay."

He did it again, but not as spectacularly. So did I – but for me it was equally as splendid.

It had been quite a weekend, and that was also when I discovered my potential as an exhibitionist.

SEVEN

I had always been an exhibitionist in private, or at least in relative privacy. I had never exposed myself for a camera, but that was what was required of me now.

"We've talked," said Angela. "You've seen a session. You've used a camera. There's only one thing left, isn't there?"

Write what you know – that was one of the "rules" of writing, although I had never obeyed it previously. The whole purpose of being in Angela's studio was so that I could write a feature on nude modelling. I could watch what happened, I could interview Dawn, but there was only one way I could really discover how it felt to be a glamour model.

That was to try it for myself.

I was never shy with men, and there had never been any reason to strip off in female company until now. Angela and Dawn were already naked, which meant I was the odd one out.

I nodded.

And I began to undress.

I was wearing sandals, a pair of jeans, a check shirt. I unbuttoned the shirt and took it off, and there was no bra beneath.

"Nice tits," said Dawn.

I unfastened my sandals and stepped out of them, unbuckled my belt, undid my zip and slid down my jeans. All I was wearing was a pair of black briefs. I thumbed them down, and then I was naked.

"Nice pubes," added Dawn. "So you're a real redhead?"

I pulled at one of my pubic curls, then let it spring back again. "That's right."

"Fiery and passionate," said Angela, as she looked me up and down. She nodded appreciatively. "I'm glad you came today, and I'm glad that model didn't turn up."

"So am I," I said, and I meant it.

I'd expected to feel uncomfortable, standing naked under the scrutiny of two other women. Perhaps if their gazes had been more critical than admiring, it wouldn't have been so easy. But I felt very relaxed. It was as if we were allies rather than competitors.

"You've gone this far," said Angela, "so shall we take some pictures?"

"Ah . . ."

"She's worried about someone she knows recognising her," said Dawn, as she stretched and stood up. She had been sitting on the bed, and now she peeled off her striped stockings and removed the cartridge belts she had been wearing. "Don't worry about that. No one ever looks at your face, just your cunt."

"These will just be test shots," Angela told me.

Dawn laughed. "That's what she tells everyone!"

Angela lashed out playfully with her foot, trying to kick Dawn's shapely backside. But Dawn was too fast, and she sprang out of range.

"It's all up to you," Angela continued. "I'll shoot off a couple of rolls of film, and you can have them. I can't use the pictures without your permission, anyway. You'd have to sign a release form first."

Angela might be honest, but that wouldn't be true of every photographer. They were no different from editors. More

104

than once I'd had my stories and articles published without agreement, without signing any contract, without any payment. The world was full of cheats and liars and crooks. If nude photos were used without my permission, it would be too late. Hiding behind a false name couldn't disguise who I was.

I asked, "What if I didn't sign, but my pictures were published?"

"You can sue me," said Angela, and then she laughed.

"What about my fee?" I asked, and I touched my breasts. "You pay by the inch, or what . . . ?"

Angela laughed again. "Turn around," she said.

I did so, and I could feel her eyes surveying me.

"Nice bum, too," said Dawn.

"We'll do a strip," Angela said to Dawn. "Get her ready."

"Ready?" I echoed. I thought I was ready. I was naked. What else did I have to do to become a nude model? "You mean ice cubes?"

Angela reached out, stroking my right breast, her index finger gliding across the hardness of my nipple. I gasped in astonishment. It was the first time a woman had ever touched me like that.

"I don't think you need any ice," she said. She glanced towards my crotch. "Or any baby oil."

I stepped back quickly, before she could reach down to make sure I needed no lubrication. But Angela turned away, rewinding the film in her camera as she gazed around the studio. It seemed she was looking for a suitable location for my pictures. She spoke to Dawn for a few seconds, who nodded and then gestured for me to follow her.

"I want to do it now," I said. If I had to wait, I might not be so willing.

"Don't rush it," Dawn told me. "It's always best to be prepared, believe me. There's far more to posing than lying back and spreading your legs."

I hoped so, because I wasn't sure I did want to spread my legs. There was a great deal of difference between nude photography and the extremes to which Dawn had gone several minutes earlier.

"Come on," she said, and I followed.

"Angie knows how to bring out the best in any girl," Dawn continued. "But you've also got to play your part, and I can help you do that. It isn't a matter of being nude, you have to be more than nude. Nudity is like innocence, because we're all born that way. Innocence is one approach, the never-been-fucked look, but it's seldom successful. And to be totally naked, you have to get dressed up. That's why Angie said you should do a strip."

We went out of the studio and into the flat, where one of the rooms was filled with all manner of exotic costumes. Sheer lingerie of every kind, all of which seemed designed to be ripped off in a frenzy of fucking; weird outfits of leather and studs, plastic and chains; every type of fancy accessory, from boots to gloves, from masks to wigs; all sorts of sex toys, from vibrators to devices whose function I couldn't even begin to guess.

"What?" I said, not really listening. I was too busy studying the amazing garments which surrounded us.

"You start with your clothes on, or most of them, and then peel off. It's always a good scenario, and Angie tries to make these things believable. You're a writer, so you should understand that. Things don't just happen. You have to explain them. Why else should a girl be naked? Because she's just taken her clothes off, right? Maybe for a shower, maybe to get changed, or maybe for a good screwing. So the series of photos will show this. The gradual unveiling and then, whammo, there's your cunt . . ."

I didn't know whether I wanted this to be "believable" or not. All I wanted was to find out what it was like to pose naked for the camera.

"And it might make it easier for you," Dawn added. "You can pretend you're stripping off for some guy."

"But I already stripped off."

"I noticed."

Dawn looked at my naked body. I looked at hers. We both laughed.

"What about you?" I said. "When Angela wanted to take some pictures of you, you just did it. You didn't have to get ready."

"I'm always ready. I'm a professional."

"But . . ."

"But nothing! You don't believe me, do you? You think that any girl can do it, can undress and be photographed? Maybe they can, but they can't do it *right*. I can. So could Angie when she was modelling. But the girls that some of the magazines use are hideous; they're worse than ugly." Dawn shook her head in disgust. "They shouldn't be allowed to undress!"

I knew what she meant from my thorough studies of the men's magazines, and I was inclined to agree.

"But even being very beautiful doesn't mean a girl is any use as a model," Dawn added. "Every girl has the right equipment. Tits, bum and twat, that's all they need, yeah?"

"Yeah," I said, taking up my cue.

"No. There's far more to it than that, believe me. I'm your average female, but I look good naked, I look good in photographs – and I look great in Angie's photos. And that's because it's my job. I'm not some amateur. When the lens focuses on me, I know exactly what to do."

I nodded, because I understood what Dawn meant. It was like writing. Anyone who could scrawl a few words on a holiday postcard thought they could be an author. And if they managed to scribble a few pages, no matter how illiterate, they assumed their prose was worthy of publication. It wasn't as easy as that, I knew. Editors wanted good writers, but they were very rare. I could believe what Dawn said about modelling. Very few people could write; very few people could model.

"I believe you," I said, and I glanced down at myself. "What about me?"

"Young, attractive, shapely." Dawn shook her head. "No chance."

"Thanks a lot."

Dawn grabbed my waist and pulled me close, hugging me as she laughed. Our naked bodies touched, her breasts pressing against mine, and her flesh felt soft and warm. There was nothing sexual about Dawn's gesture, however; she was just being friendly.

But I found it very sexual . . .

"There are millions of great girls around," said Dawn. "Go out on the street, any street, and you'll see some fantastic women. But put them in front of a camera?" She shook her head. "And yet there are other girls you'd never look at twice, and they can be an absolute knockout. Get them out of their clothes and on their backs, they're terrific. It's the magic of the camera."

Despite her claim to be average, Dawn was the type of girl who would be a knockout anywhere. I realised I'd never seen her dressed, but I knew that no one would ignore her out on the street. She possessed her own magic.

"Not just the camera," I said.

"Thank you." Dawn shrugged. "Like I said, we've all got a body. But it's what you do with it that matters, how you project yourself: everything from 'Fuck you' to 'Fuck me', from 'You can look but not touch' to 'Give it me now!' That's why I'm so good."

"Where's my tape recorder when I need it?" I said.

"Let's find something for you to put on – and then take off," said Dawn. "Wearing more means less. We can all look a lot more sexy dressed in a few items of clothes than totally naked. Or that's the theory. Shoes and stockings, transparent briefs, peephole bras, you know the kind of thing." She gestured around the bedroom boutique.

"I want to be different," I said. "Totally different."

That wasn't too difficult, because none of the stuff on offer was the kind of thing I had ever worn before. Crotchless panties and see-through bras had never formed part of my wardrobe. Underwear had always been exactly that – things I wore under my other clothes.

"You're right," Dawn agreed. "If you look different, you'll feel different, which means you'll be ready for something very different from what you've done before. Leave it to me."

By the time Dawn had finished, I literally didn't recognise myself. Instead of seeing my own image in a mirror, it was as if I were looking at someone else through a window.

It was the wig which made the most difference. I had become a blonde, with golden tresses which hung down to my shoulders. Dawn had also made up my face, putting on far more lipstick and rouge, mascara and eye shadow than I ever wore. She had seemed to overdo it, but said that was necessary for the camera. I felt almost like a china doll, my face very pale except for my gaudy lips, the circles of pink on my cheeks, and the bright blue of my eyelids. The whole shape of my face seemed different, too, because of the way Dawn had highlighted some of my features and shadowed others.

I felt very relaxed. Allowing Dawn to do my face had been very soothing. I winked at myself, and my reflection winked back at me.

"These don't match," I said, running the fingers of my right hand through my blonde hair, while I scratched my ginger public curls with my left hand.

"Easily solved," said Dawn, searching through one of the drawers of the dressing table where I sat, and she held up a razor.

"No!" Instantly, my right hand joined my left, both of them held protectively over my crotch.

Dawn laughed. "Only kidding," she said. "It really itches when it grows back, you know."

"You've done it?"

"You name it, I've done it. I had complaints after, of course, that it was like kissing a guy who was growing a beard. I asked him how he knew, but I didn't get an answer. His mouth was too busy, I suppose." Dawn licked her lips at the memory.

"But it's a myth about hair having to match up," she said. "Blondes can have darker pubic hair. Maybe not this dark." Dawn ran her fingers through her jet black curls.

She put the razor away and produced a small bottle. When unscrewed, there was a brush fitted inside the cap. It was just like a bottle of nail varnish, except it wasn't for painting fingernails . . .

"Hair dye," said Dawn.

"You mean . . . ?" I brushed my fingertips through my own pubic curls.

"It rinses out easily," said Dawn. "Yes, I've also been blonde. Shall I . . . ?"

I'd been quite content to let her paint my face, but this was a little more personal. I didn't really want Dawn to go down between my legs, seeing my cunt in closer detail than I had ever done.

"That's okay," I said, taking the bottle of dye. I smiled for a moment, thinking how crazy this seemed, and then I continued with my blonde transformation.

"I'll choose something for you to wear. I think by now I can guess your size – everywhere."

Once I'd finished lightening my pubes, the first things I put on were the black fishnet stockings Dawn had found for me; but I had a lot of trouble with the fasteners of the suspender belt.

"Never worn one before?" asked Dawn, as she helped me with the clips.

"It's like something medieval," I said.

"I know, but it's supposed to turn guys on." She stood up, tossing her hair back, her breasts jiggling as she did so. "I think it's because this is what women used to wear, so the old boys remember it as being a turn-on."

"Why not whale-bone corsets, then?" I said, trying to get the belt comfortable around my waist.

"It frames your cunt, doesn't it? The belt, the straps, the stockings. I think that's the idea. It's like a portrait." She smiled at the idea. "Anyway, it's a lot more erotic than wearing tights."

Next came the embroidered G-string, silky French

111

knickers and lacy front-fastening bra. They were a matching set, all in pink.

"My favourite colour," said Dawn. "Cunt pink."

I put them on. I'd wanted to be different, and so far everything was very different. They fitted, near enough; Dawn had been an accurate judge. The G-string was so brief it didn't cover my blonde curls, but everything was covered by the loose knickers; and the bra was so flimsy it could hardly contain my boobs.

From pink I went to black. I wore soft and feminine lingerie beneath, but tough leather on top. An old jacket, covered with badges, the slogan *Hellcat* emblazoned across the back; a tight mini-skirt; thigh length high-heeled boots; fingerless gloves; and a black helmet with a visor so dark that it acted as a mirror. As a further disguise, I wore a pair of goggles.

Dressed like that I certainly didn't recognise myself . . .

"Great," said Angela, once she saw me – and she was only referring to what I was wearing on the outside. But I was so well-covered, I could have been anyone.

She wasn't well-covered, however. Like Dawn, Angela was still naked. I envied them both; I was roasting inside my leather outfit. It would be a pleasure to strip off as quickly as possible. The theory of striptease, I guessed, was to strip as slowly as possible. There would be less strip and more tease. And for the camera the whole process might take a very long time.

"Would you like a drink?" asked Angela. "If it's your first time, it might help."

I shook my head – my helmet, I mean. I didn't need any alcohol; I was high enough already.

"It would have been nice to start with a motorbike," she said. "A couple of outside shots. But as we don't have a chopper – and no jokes please, Dawn – we'll use this." She pointed to the exercise bicycle which was part of the studio's gym set.

The area was already lit, and a camera was mounted on a tripod. She had been busy while Dawn had been getting me ready.

"On you get," she said, gesturing to the cycle.

My boots were completely impractical. I couldn't have ridden a motorbike with them, even if I knew how; it had been difficult enough walking. I clambered on the bike. It had no wheels, but the pedals were attached to a series of weights which could be adjusted to make pedalling more difficult, as if riding uphill.

I heard the first 'click' of the camera as I sat down, another as I gripped the handlebars, another as I managed to get my feet on the pedals.

"Unzip your jacket," Angela ordered.

It was the first of countless commands, some of which were:

"Take off your helmet. Turn your head. Lean back. Look to the left. Take off the jacket. Smile! Pull the skirt up. Higher. Unzip it all the way. Take it off. Unfasten the bra. Show me your left boob. Look sultry! Show me your right. Off with the bra. Turn this way. Bend over. More. More. Lean back. Back. Turn. Pout! Put the jacket back on. Leave your boobs exposed. Take off the skirt. Don't look so bored! Take off the jacket. Put the bra back on. Pull down your knickers. Blow a kiss! Let's have the goggles off. Off with the gloves. Bra unfastened. Hands over your boobs. Lick your lips! Hand inside your G-string. The other on your left breast. Now your

113

right. Look as though you're enjoying yourself! G-string down. Hand over your crotch. One arm over your boobs. Close your eyes! Lift that arm. No, the other. Fake an orgasm! Turn. Bend. Around. Down. Further. The other way. Over. Turn. Again. Turn. Look up. Turn. Look down. Bend. Back. Over. Lean. Further. Show pink . . ."

There was so much to do, so many undressings and dressings. Even after I had removed the leather skirt and my underwear, I had to put the skirt on again, leaving it unzipped to the hip, then twisting it so that the opening exposed my blonde cunt curls. The goggles and gloves kept going back on again, then off, as did the helmet. And all the time my hands would be in and out of my knickers or G-string, which were the items I kept shedding the most. The things which lasted longest were the fishnet stockings and the suspender belt, and even they had to go when it was time for just the boots. Next it was just the boots and helmet, then with the gloves. Then it was the jacket's turn to be worn again, even though I was naked below the waist. The camera click-click-clicked as I turn-turn-turned.

As well as the disrobing, a whole multitude of contortions was involved. Bending over and stretching, raising my arms, lifting my legs, throwing back my head, tossing my hair. And all the time I had to look as though I wasn't going through an ordeal. That was probably the most difficult, because the session seemed to go on for ages.

I was on and off the bike, in front of it and behind it. Lying on the floor, sitting on the floor, stretched out at an angle across both floor and bike, facing up and facing down; sitting backwards on the saddle, leaning back over the handlebars, pubis thrust upwards; raising myself up on the pedals, but leaning far forward so that my bare backside was high in the air; poised just above the saddle, with only a few pubic hairs in contact with the leather; straddling the handlebars, my outer labia sliding on either side of the metal bar.

What I thought would be the most difficult matter was the most easy. Angela told me to open my legs, wider, wider, and I did. To bend over, wider, wider, and I also did that. By this time, I simply didn't care. I did whatever was demanded of me because that meant it would all be over much sooner.

Angela came closer, closer with her camera, *click click click*, telling me what to do, and I obeyed, hardly believing what I was doing. There was nothing I hadn't done before – although perhaps not on an exercise bike, and never when two other women had been watching, a camera recording every intimate detail.

I ran my hands over my pubis, my fingers delving through the valley of my vulva, holding back the petals of my cunt, letting the bud of my clitoris grow under the lights, glistening as if with dew.

At first I assumed I was masturbating for the voyeuristic lens, but after a while I realised I was doing it for myself. Angela kept demanding that I fake an orgasm, that I should look ecstatic, that I should tense my body, let all the heat from my inner passion escape through my parted lips.

But when I finally came, I did none of those things. I exploded deep within, the tremors echoing throughout my body, but I contented myself with a quiet sigh of satisfaction.

"Thanks," said Angela.

I was hot and sweaty, and so was she. Her whole body was shining.

"I enjoyed that," she said.

There was no need for me to say the same.

But Dawn had been right. It was hard work, and it wasn't something that everyone could do; probably it wasn't something I'd want to do again. I was, however, curious to see the results. And if I'd looked so unrecognisable to myself, it didn't really matter if the photos were published.

I'd wondered what kind of girl would do nude modelling. And now I knew: a girl like me . . .

By this time all I was wearing were the boots, although I'd already had them off in order to spend a few minutes posing in the fishnet stockings. Angela's studio was full of beds, and one of those was the nearest place to sit down. It was heart-shaped, and I went across and started to pull off my boots. Dawn helped me.

"That's great!" said Angela, and there was a *click*.

As Dawn pulled off the first boot, my legs were stretched apart, my wet cunt wide open.

"Now the other," said Angela.

Dawn tugged at my other boot, studying my glistening twat as she did so. "It's a dirty job," she said, "but someone has to do it."

I burst out laughing, falling back on the bed as my boot came free. At last I had everything off and it was over. Or so I thought.

"How about the two of you?" suggested Angela.

For a moment I didn't know what she meant. But Dawn did and she threw herself down on the bed next to me. She lay by my side, as nude as I was, and she opened her legs as wide as mine.

The camera clicked.

"I want to make Angie jealous," Dawn whispered into my ear. "Let's pretend."

Her right hand slid under my neck and over my shoulder to

stroke my right breast; her left hand foraged through my damp pubic hairs. Somehow I wasn't surprised.

The camera clicked again.

But when Dawn kissed me, her tongue forcing itself between my lips, I was very surprised.

EIGHT

I was very surprised when Carl's wet tongue slid between my lips and into my mouth. I almost choked, and I pulled my head away, coughing.

He was my first "real" boyfriend and this was my first "real" kiss. I knew the theory, but I'd never expected anything quite like that. His tongue felt like a slug, all warm and slimy. Ugh . . . !

"What's the matter?" he asked.

"Nothing, nothing," I said, quickly. "I think I've got a cold coming on. You shouldn't kiss me, you might catch it."

"It'd be worth it!" he said, and he leaned forward, pulling me closer.

This time I kept my mouth firmly sealed. I'd expected that Carl would only touch his lips to mine, gently brushing his strong lips against my soft flesh, they way it was supposed to be in all the books. Instead, on the first kiss, he tried to shove his tongue all the way in.

His tongue, I supposed, was just a substitute for his cock: he wanted to push that all the way inside me, too. I found that idea somehow less repulsive than having his tongue in my mouth. I'd only recently discovered my cunt, and in a way it still wasn't a part of me. I'd probed it with my fingers, and in theory having a knob do the same wasn't really all that different. I was very particular about what I put in my mouth, however; I was always fussy about what I ate.

Carl was a year or two older than I was, and we'd met in the local library. I was borrowing family sagas, because I was on holiday. Carl was borrowing horror novels, because he was turned on by twisted violence and perverted nastiness. But I liked him enough to be sitting on his bed with him. Carl could be amusing, he had a car, he didn't look too repulsive, and I had a few weeks to kill before the next college term.

He was a lot like me; I recognised the symptoms. He was shy and had probably only been out with a few girls previously, and that was why he had taken so long to get this far. Whenever we went for a meal or to a movie, he always insisted on paying. He had never made any advances to me until now, but it seemed that tonight was the time for the account to be settled. I could see the way the balance of payments was going when he attempted to get his tongue inside my mouth and his hands inside my bra.

I wondered how experienced he was in this respect. He was probably only trying to kiss me so vigorously because this was the way other girls had kissed him. They, in turn, had learned this from other boys – and they had been taught the technique by previous girlfriends. This was the way the world went around.

We had been out to the funfair for the evening, and I had to admit to having enjoyed my share of the fun. Afterwards, he invited me back to his house for a coffee. Much to his alleged surprise, his parents were not at home. He also forgot about the coffee, and we went up in his room to listen to some music. That was something else which soon slipped his mind, as his hand slipped inside my blouse.

I didn't mind any of this, apart from the kissing. Perhaps if he'd been more subtle about it, there would have been no problem. Instead I had coughed, pulled away, and mentioned my impending cold.

"Wait a minute," I said, pushing him away with one hand,

removing his probing fingers from my blouse with the other. The way he was going he would rip the buttons off, and I hated sewing. "Don't you know what a button is?"

Carl watched in amazement as I unfastened my blouse, tugged it loose from my skirt, then took it off. His mouth hung open as he gazed at my black bra. Hesitantly, he reached for my breasts, rubbing his palms against them. Although his flesh and mine were separated by a thin layer of cotton, my nipples instantly became hard. It was the first time anyone had ever touched my tits. It was nice, very nice.

He tried to kiss me again, but I leaned away. He reached out to stop me escaping, one of his hands going around my back and trying to undo the bra strap. He had no success, and after several seconds his other hand joined in the attempt. But he still had no idea what he was doing; but I knew all he was doing was ruining the elastic.

"I'll do it," I told him.

He was reluctant to give up his endeavours. I noticed the bulge in his crotch, and so I reached for his zip.

"Hey!" Carl pulled back rapidly. He looked amazed.

"What's wrong?" I asked, and I took off my bra.

His mouth was even wider than before, his eyes staring. He was obviously surprised and he shook his head, unable to say anything. Slowly, he reached out to touch my bare breasts, almost as if he didn't believe what he was seeing. He stroked my naked flesh, his palms circling both nipples, gradually spiralling towards them, lightly caressing them with his fingertips. It felt nice, very nice.

"Why don't you get your cock out?" I suggested.

Carl's hands suddenly stopped rubbing my boobs and he gazed at me in astonishment.

"What?" he said, as though he hadn't heard.

"I can see it wants to get out," I said, nodding towards the very apparent lump in his denims. "I'd like to see it."

"What?" he repeated.

"You know what," I told him. "Show me your prick, and you can touch my tits again." I took hold of his wrists and removed his hands. "But if you don't want to . . ." I reached for my discarded bra.

"No," he said. "Yes, I mean."

He looked at me, I nodded encouragement, and he tugged at the metal button at the top of his jeans, then slowly pulled down his zip. It seemed he didn't want to do it, which I couldn't understand. A vertical shape became visible within the fabric of his bright yellow shorts. He eased the elastic waistband over the bulge, and the purple head of his knob came into view.

"All of it," I ordered.

For a moment I thought Carl would refuse, but then he stood up. His jeans dropped to his ankles, and he pushed his shorts down to his knees. His hard cock was only the second one I had ever seen, and I studied it with fascination. It seemed shorter than James's penis had been, although fatter. As I watched, it was still growing slightly, the glans stretching free from the foreskin; the testicles were already drawn up tight. The whole apparatus was two feet away from me, at about eye level. I could easily have reached out and touched it; I was both tempted and scared of doing so.

Unlike James, Carl seemed embarrassed and I wondered how to put him at his ease. I decided to take off the rest of my clothes, so that he'd also have something to look at. Only a few seconds had passed since his erection had come into view. I stood up, unzipped the side of my skirt and allowed it to fall to the ground. I'd already kicked off my sandals before sitting on Carl's bed, and so all I was now wearing was a pair of black briefs.

Carl was staring at my panties, and I was about to thumb them down, when he suddenly grabbed for his prick.

"Uhhhhhhh," he groaned.

He was too late, because his tool began to spurt, spraying spunk into the air. I'd thought a man could only climax through manipulating his cock, either sliding it in and out of a cunt, or by jerking off. But Carl had achieved spontaneous orgasm. I was very impressed, and I'd also learned something new.

He turned away, holding his erupting dick; but his semen oozed out between his fingers and dripped down his hands. He left the room as quickly as he could, which wasn't very fast because he was hobbled by the jeans around his ankles, and he couldn't get them off because of his shoes.

I wondered whether to take off my briefs, or whether to wait until Carl returned. I sat down on the bed again, then lay back. Almost without my noticing, my right hand slipped inside my panties. Carl's demonstration must have been more arousing than I had realised, and I unhurriedly fingered myself. Carl's orgasm hadn't been totally spontaneous, I supposed: it had been triggered by seeing me half naked. Thinking of my effect on him, I brought myself off once, and was dreamily going for seconds while wondering what would happen when Carl returned.

When he came back, he saw where my hand was, but he said, "How do you like your coffee?"

Which was when I suspected very little would happen, that plus the fact he was fully dressed.

"Black, with brown sugar," I told him.

He went out again, heading along the corridor. I followed, wearing just my black cotton briefs.

"Something wrong?" I asked, as we entered the kitchen.

"No." He filled the kettle.

"Why don't you take your clothes off again?"

He looked at me, trying to keep his eyes on mine. He failed, instead focusing on my bare boobs. He tried to keep a straight face, with an equal lack of success.

He smiled as he looked me up and down, and he shook his head.

"You're just too . . . too experienced," he said. "I'm . . . er . . . not used to a girl like you." He laughed. "You've got to be gentle with me."

I also laughed, although for a different reason.

We went back upstairs, where we drank our coffee and listened to CDs. I let Carl kiss me. Now I knew what to expect, I discovered I could get to like it. But I kept my knickers on, and I didn't try to get his clothes off again.

I'd been rushing things. Maybe I shouldn't have undressed until we had been out more often – and stayed in more often. Or maybe I was supposed to be more reluctant about stripping off. Or maybe it was Carl who should have removed my bra. Maybe anything. I had a lot to learn, and I'd already learned that I ought to take things more slowly.

One step at a time. I'd let him touch my clothed tits, then allowed him to see my bare tits, then permitted him to feel my naked tits. Next, I discovered, came the part where he licked my nipples, sucking at them in turn, drawing them into his mouth and teasing them with his tongue. And that was very nice indeed.

We would have proceeded further, but then Carl's parents returned home and I had to dress very quickly.

123

I'd seen penises become erect, watched them being stimulated, observed them ejaculate. The next stage in my education, I knew, would involve more than just looking.

But Carl and I never did get any further together. He had begun to bore me and we had nothing much in common. Although I'd been interested in his prick, that wasn't something exclusive to him. Every guy possessed one, so I might as well take my next lessons from someone who was more intelligent and more fun.

There seemed to be no hurry, and I had other matters which deserved my attention. The only thing I wanted to go to bed with was a good book, and there was always plenty to read.

By this time, I was in my first year at college, so there was also plenty of work to do. The senior male students were all drawn to the new input of girls, like feral predators hunting down their helpless victims. But it wasn't only the males who were fuck-happy. Some of the new girls went cock-crazy. Away from home for the first time in their lives, they screwed and sucked a different man every night. Sometimes two or three.

While I read a different book every night. Two or three at weekends.

I had plenty of offers, for a drink, alcoholic or otherwise, to concerts, rock and classical, to movies and the theatre, even to football matches. And some such offers were accepted. A few times I even went as far as I'd progressed with Carl. I had my tits groped and licked, but I was always careful not to be too forward. It wasn't up to me to undo my bra strap, even though it would have saved a lot of time. Nor was it my role to remove my sweater or blouse or T-shirt, which meant it was usually only pushed up over my breasts while my boobs were sucked and stroked.

I must have been going wrong somewhere, because I was sure this wasn't happening to other girls on my course. They'd long gone past the stage of only having their tits licked. I tried not to let it bother me, and I kept on studying; but when the others had their heads down it was unlikely to be in a book.

So the time went by, until an end of term paper was due and there was a book I needed to read. It had already been taken out of the library by Tim, one of the guys on my course, and someone else had reserved it next. Tim read even more than I did. He always wore an old sports jacket and a college scarf wrapped around his neck, even indoors.

"When will you be finished with 'The Annotated Haworth Diaries?' " I asked after one of the seminars.

"I have to return it to the library tomorrow morning," said Tim.

"That's not what I asked. When will you be finished with the book?"

"Half past seven."

I hadn't expected such a precise answer. "Can you lend it to me overnight?"

Tim blinked at me through his glasses, and he frowned.

I smiled at him. "Please."

"Very well." He nodded. "You can have it if you come and get it." If any other guy had expressed himself that way, he would have been implying something completely different; but from Tim there was no trace of innuendo.

"Half past seven?" I said.

"Half past seven," he replied, and he told me where I could find his room.

He lived in one of the halls of residence opposite my own, but it was almost eight o'clock when I knocked on the door. I'd had a shower and washed my hair, for my benefit not Tim's, and it was later than I thought. I tucked my wet hair inside a woollen hat, pulled on coat, scarf and boots, then hurried over. Tim had always seemed very meticulous, almost fussy, and I hoped my lack of punctuality wouldn't alter his decision to lend me the book.

"Come in!"

I turned the handle and did so. His room was almost exactly the same as my own, furnished with only a bed, set of drawers, wardrobe, desk and a chair. But it seemed smaller than mine because there were books and papers and files and documents everywhere. I'd thought my room was untidy until I saw Tim's.

He was bent over the desk, scribbling notes. I closed the door behind me and waited until he glanced around. It was the first time I'd seen him without his sports jacket and scarf. He was wearing a white shirt and a tie, which must always have been hidden by the jacket and scarf that now hung on the back of the door. His leather shoes gleamed with polish, and his dark trousers were sharply creased.

"Yes?" he said, leaning towards me as if I were too far away for him to see.

"I've come for the book," I reminded him. "The *Diaries*. Remember? Have you finished with them?"

"Yes." He nodded. "Yes." He glanced around, searching for the book, his head still nodding. "Yes, yes."

"Is that it?" I recognised the volume and walked across the room, picking it up from the floor by the desk.

"Yes," he agreed, "yes."

"Thanks," I said. "Shall I give it to you tomorrow morning, or shall I take it back to the library?"

"Yes."

"Which?"

Unable to say "yes" for the ninth time, he simply shrugged. He seemed nervous having me in his room, and so I tucked the book under my arm and headed for the door.

"Would you . . . er . . . like . . . er . . . a coffee?" he asked.

With almost anyone else, that would mean something different and there would be no chance of a coffee. I hesitated a moment, and Tim glanced away.

"You don't have to," he muttered.

I guessed what an effort it had probably been for him to invite me, and I said, "Yes."

He turned towards me again, leaning forwards, frowning as if he hadn't heard me properly.

"Yes," I repeated. "I'd love a coffee. Thanks."

Tim jumped to his feet, knocking various papers from the desk in his haste, hurrying to fix the coffee before I could change my mind. What I'd said was true. I did want a coffee. It was cold out, and I needed something hot inside to warm me up. But I didn't say that, even to Tim.

"Sit down," he said. "Take your hat and coat off."

I could have sat on the bed, but I decided against that. Instead I moved the chair away from the desk, because I didn't want to appear as though I was looking at Tim's notes. Pushing a few books aside with my foot, I set the chair back on the floor where it was still close enough for me to see what Tim had been writing, and I sat down. I kept my hat and coat on.

"How do you like it?" he asked.

"Black, please. Have you any brown sugar?"

"That's the way I take it. Black and brown. One sugar?"

"One," I echoed.

While Tim made the coffee, I pretended to look at the book but was really peering at his notes. He must have noticed what I was doing, because he said, "If you want, I could tell you about the 'Diaries', save you having to read them all tonight."

"Oh, yes, good idea," I said, and it was. "Thanks."

"Maybe you can do something for me sometime. Here."

"Thanks," I said again, taking the coffee.

"Take your coat off," he said again.

That wasn't such a good idea, but I did take off my hat. I shook my hair free; it was still very damp. It was warm in the room and my hair should soon dry. Tim looked at me, all wrapped up in my thick coat and college scarf, identical to his, and he shrugged. He sat on the edge of the bed and reached for the book I was holding.

"May I?"

I passed it to him, then crossed my legs. My long coat came open, baring my right leg halfway up the thigh. I quickly uncrossed my legs again, but Tim hadn't noticed. He was busy flicking through the book with one hand. His cup was held loosely in the other hand, and a trickle of coffee dripped to the floor every time he turned a page.

"Here," he said. "These are the chapters which bear most relevance to our paper."

"But if you tell me all this, won't what we write be too similar?"

"Not at all, not at all. Literary criticism has nothing to do with facts, does it? We all view the same thing differently; everything is a matter for interpretation." Tim lifted his coffee to his lips. Most of it was on the floor, but he didn't notice. He drained the cup, then said, "Listen . . ."

He began to read, his voice low but confident, using different inflections to emphasise various sections, then breaking off to make certain points.

I listened attentively, and I was impressed. Tim was much better than many of our lecturers. He knew what was important, that learning wasn't a matter of cramming everything into the memory but of how to develop that knowledge oneself. I asked for a pen and paper so I could make notes. Although I lost all sense of time as he read, I gradually realised I was getting hotter and hotter.

"Can you turn the radiator down?" I asked, when he paused and glanced up to see if I understood the point he had been making.

"Take your coat off."

"I can't."

"Can't?"

"I haven't got anything on underneath."

He laughed a moment, obviously not believing me. It was true, however. Realising that I was late, I'd literally pulled on my hat and coat, scarf and boots, that was all. I only intended to pick up a book – that was all.

"I don't mind," said Tim.

I could have endured the heat, I could have left. I did neither. At least I could pretend I was taking Tim at his word . . .

I had unwrapped my scarf earlier, but now I wound it around my neck again. It was long and it was wide, and it hung down in front of me as I unfastened the buttons of my coat.

Tim was pretending to study the book, but I could see his eyes were really on me.

I slipped the coat off my shoulders and stood naked in front of him. The book crashed to the floor. Tim stared, his eyes wide through the lenses of his glasses.

All I wore were my knee-length red suede boots and my college scarf, but the scarf was draped over all my vital areas. It was wide enough to cover my breasts from nipple to nipple, long enough to cover my pubis.

Tim opened his mouth to speak, then shook his head when he could find no words. He reached down to pick up the dropped book, but his eyes were still focused on me, and his probing hand was unable to find it again. He gave up, coughed, then said, "I told you I didn't mind." And he smiled.

Until that moment I had been unsure of how he would react, but now I also smiled. So far he had seen nothing, not really. Things could end like that if necessary.

"Shall I put my coat back on?" I asked.

His arm went down again, hunting for the dropped book. He was still smiling. "You're not leaving, are you? We haven't finished."

No, I thought, we haven't.

I sat down, my bare bum on the seat of the chair. The scarf hid my breasts, more or less, and hung down between my legs. I wondered how long Tim would be able to concentrate. He located the book, picked it up, and began turning the pages. I could tell he'd have difficulty finding his place, because the volume was upside down.

While he was doing that, I pulled my boots off, then drew my feet up on the chair and I sat cross-legged. The scarf still modestly masked my crotch, hanging down between my legs, but it had become twisted and now hung between my exposed boobs.

"Yes," said Tim, finally, "yes. As I was saying, the breast thing about . . . er . . . the best thing, I mean . . ."

He wiped his forehead with the back of his sleeve, then resumed reading. As he did so, he unfastened the buttons of his shirt, and it was almost as if he didn't know what he was doing. Tim had been holding the book across his lap, but I could see that it was slightly higher than it had been. Something seemed to be pushing it up . . .

He was trying to take off his shirt, but one hand was still holding one edge of the book, and he'd forgotten to undo the cuff buttons or remove his tie. Meanwhile, he kept on reading, but by now he was hesitating and his voice was no longer so confident. I'd no idea whether what he was reading even made sense, because I was no longer listening.

"That's enough for tonight," I told him.

"Oh . . . are you leaving?"

"You want me to?"

He shook his head slowly, and slowly he smiled.

I also smiled as I stood up, took the book from his hand, put it on the floor, unfastened the cuff buttons and helped him off with his shirt and tie. He did not resist; nor did he try to prevent me from unhooking his belt and unzipping his pants; but neither did he try to help me. I couldn't get his trousers down because of his shoes, so I pulled those off first, then eased his trousers down.

I was kneeling on the floor between his legs, gazing at the vertical shape which thrust itself up through the fabric of his pants.

"Enjoying yourself?" I asked.

"Yes, very much."

I climbed on the bed next to him, and he put his hands on my shoulders, drawing me towards him. He kissed the tip of my nose, and I wondered if his sight really was that bad, but a moment later his hands managed to find my breasts without any trouble. We toppled over together and lay side by side. Tim's lips located my left nipple, drawing it into his mouth, while one of his hands occupied itself with my right breast and the other stroked my buttocks. I was enjoying what he was doing, but thought that I should be contributing something, and so my right hand slid down his side, through the elastic of his waistband, and then slowly moved around.

I knew exactly what I was aiming for, and I found it: Tim's cock.

At first I touched it lightly with my fingertips, measuring its dimensions. It felt enormous, and I wondered how such a thing could possibly ever fit into a cunt. But from what I had already observed, I knew that Tim's knob was no larger than James's and Carl's pricks had been. I ran my fingers around the balls, through the wiry pubic hairs, then up the shaft, gliding lightly over the dome. Finding a bead of liquid at the very tip, I quickly retreated, wiping my fingers on Tim's pants.

He thrust his hips forward, encouraging me to continue. I didn't have much choice, because my hand was trapped between his body and mine. Meanwhile, he had transferred his oral attention to my right nipple, his hand now caressing my left breast.

I slipped my hand under Tim's testicles, cupping them in my palm, surprised that I could feel both of the egg-shapes. But as I touched them, his balls drew up, the scrotum tightening. I slid my fingers higher, my thumb and fingers separating as they went around the base of the shaft. Then for the first time ever I took hold of a penis, gripping the firm flesh, feeling its warmth, its vitality.

My heart had been pounding furiously, but now I detected

a different pulse. I could feel the blood throbbing through the solid maleness, and its pace seemed to match my own. My hand made a fist and I slid it slowly up towards the glans.

"Yes," said Tim, removing his mouth from my tit for a moment, "yes."

It was what he wanted me to do; it was what I wanted to do; but I couldn't get much leverage, being only able to move my wrist; and neither could I see. I let go and pulled my right arm, trying to release it. Tim understood, and he rolled on his back. While he quickly pushed down his pants, kicking them free and also deftly discarding his socks, I sat up. Then he lay back and looked up at me, waiting.

I examined his erection. There was no loose skin near the head; Tim had been circumcised. This was another first for me. I touched the shaft again, running my fingers from the base to the tip, then back again, before taking a firm grip once more.

And I began to masturbate him, sliding my hand up and down his virile length. Tim closed his eyes as I did so. I moved nearer for a better view of what I was doing. I remembered how James had spat into his hand for lubrication, and I leaned even nearer. Tim's eyes opened as he felt my hot breath on his skin. I could smell the heady aroma of his blatant manhood, and I opened my mouth, allowing a ball of saliva to drip onto the purple dome, before moving back again, propping myself up on one elbow as I lay next to Tim. He closed his eyes again, luxuriating in the sybaritic treatment I was bestowing upon him.

I wanted to ask if I was doing it correctly, although I didn't want him to know this was my first time, but it seemed he had no complaints. He was clearly enjoying himself. I must have known what to do instinctively, and I discovered I was having fun pleasuring him. I was also aroused, my vaginal lips moist, my clitoris swollen.

My hand stroked up and down, slowly, up and down, more speedily. Tim was lying back, relaxed, but after perhaps a minute his limbs abruptly tensed and I felt a trembling in his shaft. His orgasm was imminent, I knew. Remembering what I had previously witnessed, I didn't want too be too close to the source of the eruption; but by holding on, I would continue to be a part of what was happening.

Neither could I have let go, because suddenly Tim's hand was on mine, clutching it tight, making it stop its rhythmic pumping. Because of the angle of my hand, I'd been holding his cock towards me, and the glans was still aimed in my direction when the shaft shot suddenly the first foaming spurt of spunk.

I watched in fascination as the creamy jet squirted from Tim's dick – and landed on the scarf which I was still wearing. The second pulse also hit my scarf, although lower down. Judging the trajectory, I calculated that the third geyser would splash against my flesh. Instead, I caught it on the scarf. I did the same with the fourth spurt. The subsequent ejaculations were insignificant, in both distance and quantity.

Going to college was more than academic learning. Different people, different places, different experiences – they were all part of my education.

Tim sighed ecstatically and relaxed. His hand still held mine, and I felt his cock begin to wilt like a flower after it had blossomed. After several seconds, he opened his eyes and looked at me. He released my hand, and I unwound my freshly silvered scarf. When I left, I decided, I would exchange Tim's scarf for mine.

Tim sat up and surveyed my body, totally nude for the first time.

"Now it's your turn," he told me.

I knew exactly what he meant, and I was both terrified and excited.

"Lie down," he ordered, and I obeyed.

He rested his right hand on my chest, immediately beneath my breasts, and slowly he slid it down across my damp flesh, down over my navel, down over my stomach, down, down, down into the nest of my pubic hairs. My thighs had been clenched together, but at his touch I parted my legs.

His index finger found the valley which led down, down, towards my vagina, and it slipped down, down into the secret heart of my being.

That brief instant of contact was all that was necessary.

I came instantly, my whole body exploding convulsively, and I cried out with absolute pleasure as I climaxed again and again.

It was the first time anyone else had touched my cunt.

NINE

And this was the first time another girl had touched my cunt.

Angela could see that Dawn's fingers were stroking my vulva, and it was probably what she wanted, because I heard the click of the camera shutter. But because Dawn's long black hair veiled our faces, the photographer would be unable to see that her lips were against mine, her tongue probing my mouth.

Despite my initial surprise, I returned Dawn's kiss, my own lips and tongue responding with equal fervour. And my hand reached down, trying to find her cunt.

But before I was able to more than brush my fingertips across her pubic hairs, Dawn suddenly pulled away, withdrawing both her mouth and her hand, and she laughed.

Had she really intended to make Angela jealous? Or had that simply been an excuse? I wondered if this was some other bizarre game of theirs, or whether she had retreated before Angela noticed the intensity of our brief passion. There was no malice in the laughter, however; Dawn was laughing with me, not at me.

I touched my fingers to my lips, remembering her kiss, the forbidden taste of another female mouth upon my own. It had only lasted a few brief seconds, and it was that brevity which I regretted – not the fact that I'd consented to the kiss. A few hours earlier I would have found the idea of kissing another girl completely alien. But much had happened in those last few hours. I'd done so many things I never imagined I either could or would, displaying myself so shamelessly for the camera.

Dawn and I were still lying side by side, our shoulders touching, our hips touching, our thighs touching. Our legs were both outspread, with Dawn's right leg crossed over my left, and Angela was studying us through the lens.

"Don't just lie there," she said. "Do something!"

"What do you want?" asked Dawn, and she yawned as though the whole thing bored her.

But I knew she hadn't been bored when we kissed, and neither had I been. I wanted to do it again. I wanted her to touch my cunt – and I wanted to touch hers. Angela's request that we pose would be the ideal excuse for our tongues to intertwine once more, for Dawn's fingers to find my eager twat, for mine to venture into another girl's hot cunt for the first time.

"Go through a double routine," said Angela

"What's that?" I asked, although I had my hopes.

"We do exactly the same thing," said Angela. "Blonde and brunette. Two cunts are more than twice as erotic as one, that's the theory. Like now, with both our legs apart."

"Turn over," Angela said. "Bums in the air."

We obeyed. Side by side, we knelt on the bed and thrust our buttocks as high as we could.

"Legs wider."

We opened our legs, opened our cunts. That was all we were – bums and twats, because nothing else could be seen of us. Then Angela had us on the floor bending double, looking upside down through our legs.

"Legs wider," came the inevitable order.

This time we were bums and twats and inverted faces.

Then we lay on our backs, thrusting our hips in the air,

137

and all that could be seen were our gaping cunts, side by side. Our backs still to the ground, Dawn moved over me, supporting her weight with her hands, and now our pouting twats were above one another. Then we turned completely over, and this time I was on top, and Angela photographed just our taut buttocks and glistening labia.

"Tit to tit," said Angela, and we went into another contortion.

Dawn was still beneath me, but now we were facing each other, our cunts touching. We ground our hips together, our breasts and nipples were pressed tight between us. Angela took another few shots of our bums and open vaginal lips. Because of her position, she was unable to see that we were kissing, our lips rubbing wetly, our tongues exploring each other's mouth.

Apart from those few seconds, I could understand why Dawn had yawned. After so much posing on my own, I felt tired and a bit fed up, yet I was also very stimulated by the proximity of Dawn's nude body – and, as always, by the voyeuristic gaze of Angela's camera. As she squatted down to take pictures of our contortions, her own twat came into full view for the first time, the inner labia parted as she thrust out one of her legs to maintain her balance. It seemed that she needed no baby oil to make her cunt lips gleam.

"Okay," she said, reloading the camera. "Let's have a bit of touching up, but keep it soft."

By now I was getting the hang of the jargon, that "soft" meant simulation or not going very far. How far was far, however, I wasn't sure. The line between "soft" and "hard" seemed totally arbitrary – and totally unnecessary.

"Is this alright by you?" asked Dawn.

"If it wasn't," I said, "I wouldn't do it. It's all research, isn't it?" It was my turn to laugh.

Dawn nodded. "After all," she said, "we're only pretending." She managed not to laugh.

When we lay down on the bed together and she licked my left nipple, drawing it into her mouth and washing it with her saliva, I wondered how she behaved when she wasn't pretending. But for me the feeling was sensational.

After taking a couple of shots of Dawn's lips on my breast, I noticed that Angela lowered the camera and watched us for a few seconds. It seemed she had her own doubts about where the line between fantasy and reality should be drawn, and she was uncertain whether Dawn was deliberately going beyond that limit.

"What should I do?" I asked.

I had become used to obeying her commands. It was like being back at school, doing what teacher said. It was as if I couldn't be blamed for what I did because I was only following my instructions. I'd exposed my wet cunt to the camera's inquisitive eye because that was my function as a glamour model.

"Do whatever you want," replied Angela, watching as Dawn continued to suckle on my tit. Then her eyes met mine, and she knew I had never been in this situation before. "Whatever feels good," she added. She smiled, giving her permission for me to do whatever I wished with Dawn. "I can always censor the pictures." She raised the camera, ready for whatever I did.

'Whatever I want.' But I wasn't sure what I wanted. 'Whatever feels good.' And until I tried it, I didn't know what felt good.

"And can I do whatever I want?" asked Dawn, as her

lips finally released the nipple which she had kept such a pampered prisoner.

I was unable to fathom what kind of game they were playing. All I knew was that a totally desirable body lay next to mine. It didn't matter that Dawn was female, that I'd never done any of this before. Reaching out, I put my hand on her bare breast.

I'd touched my own boobs countless times, when I was washing and when I was wanking, but to touch one which belonged to another girl was absolutely different. I felt both the softness of her flesh and the firmness of the nipple, and the warmth of her whole body flowed up through my hand and arm, radiating throughout my whole being.

I wanted to hold her, to hug her, to kiss her, to caress her, to love her. And I did.

As my hands stroked Dawn's breasts, it was her turn to lie back and enjoy my tender touch. I heard the click of the camera, but it had no relevance to what I was doing. Dawn's nipples were darker than mine, the areolae wider and more dimpled, and I was fascinated by the difference. I held back as long as I could, but then my mouth engulfed one of her nipples, greedily sucking and licking at the firm flesh. I heard Dawn sigh with pleasure, and she ran her fingers over my back.

After that, I hardly knew what I was doing – or what was being done to me. My hands explored Dawn's soft body, stroking and caressing, and she was doing the same to me, her fingers sensuously flowing over my flesh. Although I was lost in passion, Dawn was far less inhibited than I was, and so it was her fingers which first directed themselves upon my cunt. She stroked my pubic mound, then moved deeper, fingertips gliding across my clitoris. Her touch was electrifying.

Who could know how to satisfy a woman better than a woman? Dawn had a cunt of her own and thus knew exactly how to provoke the most stimulating response in another girl, and my arousal became even more heightened.

I held her tighter, pressing her whole body against mine, and my own hand found her twat at the same time as our lips rediscovered each other. We kissed, mouths opening in simultaneous surrender as our invading tongues advanced. A tongue was a tongue, it didn't matter what sex it was.

Then my index finger slid between Dawn's legs, into the moistness of her labia, instantly finding the tiny bud that was her clitoris. It grew at my touch.

There was no pretence on my part and there could have been none from Dawn. The camera was forgotten, Angela was forgotten, all that mattered was the two of us.

Who needed a man? Who needed a cock?

I was fucking, I realised – fucking another girl . . . !

And that thought was enough to send me spiralling even higher into orbit.

Dawn fingered my cunt while I fingered hers, and our pleasure seemed to increase exponentially as we each brought the other to greater heights. I tried to hold back as long as I could, not wanting to climax, because the longer I waited the more stupendous would be my orgasm. Our fingers worked frantically, our tongues melding to the same climactic rhythm – but then suddenly it was gone, we were torn apart.

Dawn's magical fingers vanished from my twat, my own hand was dragged away from her wondrous cunt, even our lips were drawn apart. We were being forcibly separated.

My eyes had been closed as if asleep, as if enjoying the most amazing wet dream of my life. But now I awoke, both angry and disappointed by the abrupt denial of a proper resolution to our relationship, and I saw Angela pulling us apart. We had succeeded in making her jealous.

Angela came between myself and Dawn – but only because she joined us on the bed, her lithe body writhing between us, warm and damp and burning with lust . . .

A few seconds earlier, I had one pair of hands exploring my body, one pair of lips kissing mine. But now there were four inquisitive hands touching me, two pairs of passionate lips roving over my naked body.

The other two could have kissed and stroked each other, but it was evident that I was the focal point of their attention. They already knew each other intimately. For them I was a novelty, a new body to lick and caress, to fondle and finger.

The dream returned, sweeping me into a living erotic fantasy.

I wanted to respond, to touch their bodies while they touched mine. For a while I was able to stroke Angela's breasts, to feel how different they were from Dawn's, how the texture of her skin was dissimilar, and how even her pubic hairs were not the same.

But there were two of them, only one of me, and I was helpless to resist. I became their obedient sex slave. And I was the most willing of victims. I lay back languidly as they subjected me to all manner of exquisite physical delights. My whole body became an erogenous zone.

One of them sucked and licked my left nipple, while the other directed the divine attention of her lips and tongue to my other breast. Meanwhile, my limbs were being stroked, my whole body caressed and fondled. I was sensually overwhelmed, unable to move, to react, to speak, to do anything except absorb all the pleasure which was being inflicted on my supine body.

Every inch of my flesh received the gift of their affection, the touch of their fingers or their lips. I felt a tongue lapping between my toes, which under other circumstances would have produced only laughter; but at that moment, it was the quintessence of total pleasure.

Even in my languid heaven of bliss, I realised there was one part of my anatomy which both Dawn and Angela had avoided. They would go only so near, then retreat, their fingertips drawing back, teasing me with a promise which had yet to be fulfilled.

I had no idea how much time had past, but I knew my lonely cunt had not been touched since Dawn's fingers had so suddenly been drawn away.

Throughout all this I had been rising higher and higher on a swollen tide of utter joy, but now the flood threatened to overwhelm me. Held back and denied release, it seemed I would never escape from my physical constraints.

I was pinned down, unable to move my limbs, unable to grant myself the escape which I craved. Instead, Dawn and Angela carried me even higher and higher, towards an ultimate of which I had never previously dreamed.

My whole body twitched and trembled, and I began to moan as the waves of pleasure reached yet a new peak.

But then I was silenced. A mouth closed upon mine, lips to lips, tongue to tongue. We breathed the same air, she and I, and I didn't even know if it was Dawn or Angela who was kissing me.

Which meant I didn't know if it was Angela or Dawn who kissed my cunt . . .

I felt the warmth of her breath on my vulva, and a moment

143

later her tongue was lapping between my labia, fixing itself upon my clitoris, licking and sucking, sucking and licking.

And I came. And came. And came.

My whole body erupted in a cataclysmic frenzy, and the other two were unable to hold me down any longer.

I was consumed by the pyrotechnic flares which exploded from the incandescence of my vagina, consuming every atom of my body in a spectacular blaze. My whole being was destroyed in the raging flames of my orgasm – but out of the ashes I was born anew.

I sighed, allowing the heat to escape from my trembling lips. I was aglow, bathed in sweat, totally drained. My eyes remained closed, and all I wanted to do was lie where I was, drift away into slumber, savouring the memory.

But I was allowed no respite. Two pairs of hands still stroked my body, two pairs of lips still kissed my damp flesh. These were the kisses of life, invigorating me. Now it was my turn to repay the debt.

Slowly, I gained control of my limbs once again. In a few seconds I would be able to fondle breasts and buttocks, to lick nipples and navels, to play my role in the threesome of which I had become a part.

Then I sensed a face descending towards mine, and I opened my mouth to receive the kiss which was being bestowed upon me. It was Angela, I knew immediately. Her lips were different, her tongue was different. I knew Dawn's smell, her intimate aroma. I kissed Angela for the first time, our lips pressed tight, our tongues intertwining.

I sensed Angela's own personal odour, but there was another very familiar scent on her lips and on her tongue. It took me a few seconds to recognise what it was.

It was my private aroma – the smell of my own twat . . .

Angela had licked me out, and now the flavour was being returned to me – and it was as if I was tasting my own cunt.

Once again I climaxed, shuddering in absolute ecstasy.

"So you went and saw Angela?" asked Don.

"Yes."

"And?"

"And what?"

"Was it worth it? Did you get an interview? Was she cooperative?"

"It was worth it," I said, and I couldn't help but smile. "She was very cooperative."

"Are you going to tell me about it?"

"There's nothing much to tell." Then I laughed. "Read my article!"

Don and I were together for one of our regular meetings, having a drink while we checked up on what each other had been doing lately, and offering advice and congratulations or sympathy. Don had been even less punctual than usual, and I was on my second drink by the time he arrived.

"There must be something you can tell me," Don insisted. "Something you haven't written about."

"Nothing of much interest," I said, shrugging. "I went and saw Angela, we talked. Then I talked to one of her models. It was just a job, just an interview, that's all."

Don nodded, but I could tell he didn't believe me.

And even if I'd told him what had really happened, he wouldn't have believed me.

I'd kept thinking of the photos which Angela had taken and what would happen to them. If she used the pictures without my permission, I'd be unlikely to find out. How different did I really look with a blonde wig? What if the photos ended up in one of the magazines for which Don worked – and he was asked to write the captions? Would he recognise me?

By the very end of our session, there could be no doubt who I was. The wig had fallen off, and the blonde dye on my pubic hair had gone, washed away by sweat and saliva and come. Whether any pictures had been taken at the end of my encounter with Angela and Dawn, I'd been too lethargic to notice; but it wouldn't have surprised me.

Probably nothing would surprise me any more.

There were no regrets, however. It was all experience, all data to my stacked in my memory files, to be filtered out and used in my writing. Precise memories of what had occurred were very hazy, almost as if I had been drunk. But I suppose I'd been high in a completely different way, peaking on absolute sensuality and total abandon.

It was a day never to be forgotten, even though I had forgotten so much of it. Had I really done 'that' . . . ? Did I really let them do 'that' to me . . . ?

I licked at my lips, remembering. I noticed Don watching, and so I took a mouthful of my drink.

But I still remembered the taste of cunt. My own. And then Dawn's. And Angela's. No wonder guys were so keen on cunnilingus. It was just so, so nice.

"What about you?" I asked, bringing myself back to the present. "What's the latest on the movie deal?"

"Don't change the subject," said Don. "What's happened to you? You're different somehow. What is it?"

"Nothing," I insisted, and I took another drink so I didn't have to say any more. I'd always been impressed by Don's awareness, but now I wished he was as unobservant as most other people.

"You're not seeing someone are you?" he asked. He

stared at me, and he seemed to be gazing right into my thoughts, knowing exactly what had happened a few days ago in Angela's studio.

But what if he did know? How would he react? Judging by what I'd read in the men's magazines, the male of the species was fascinated by the idea of females having sex together. If a girl went off with another man, it could provoke violence; but lesbianism seemed to be no threat. Girls could play together all they wanted, because as soon as a real man appeared they would bow to his command. According to theory, no woman could resist a cock.

I shook my head and smiled, and I reached out to put my hand on top of Don's. "No," I assured him, "you're the only man in my life."

"So when can I put some life into you?" he asked, gripping my hand, winking lasciviously with deliberate over-emphasis.

"How's the movie deal?" I asked again, and I expected his usual enthusiastic response.

Instead Don slowly shook his head and stared into his glass. "I've been thinking of getting a job," he said, softly.

"But you've got a job," I told him. "You're a writer!"

"No. I've been kidding myself for too long. It's time to join the real world."

He smiled, but I'd never seen him look so sad.

When we left, for the first time ever he didn't ask me to go home with him. For the first time I would have agreed, but I didn't offer. I didn't want to be turned down, and from the mood Don was in I knew that would have been his inevitable response.

I made my way home, and all the time I was thinking about Don. I'd been on a real high recently, and suddenly I was down. I should have insisted I went back with him, or that he came home with me. Even if it was only for a short while, I could have made him forget. What kind of a friend was I?

I awoke to the insistent ringing of the telephone, and I was still half-asleep when I picked it up.

"Hello," I said. "Yes, speaking. Oh, yes, hello. Thanks for phoning."

It was Jeff, the editor who had asked me to write the article on nude models.

"I like a writer who can deliver promptly," he said.

"And I like an editor who reads promptly," I said, which I thought was a very good response considering how exhausted I was.

After leaving Don, I'd stayed up reading and gone to bed very late. Even then I had been awake a long time, thinking about what he'd said. Getting a job? I'd often considered that myself, although never for long – only until the next overdue fee arrived. But if Don was thinking about giving up writing, things must have been really bad for him. He didn't want to stay on the treadmill, churning out formula hack work. That was okay for a while, but if he couldn't move up the ladder he wanted out.

From where I stood, I could see the clock. It was half past ten. I never knew editors started work so early.

"This is great stuff," said Jeff. "I'm very pleased. It's much better than I even hoped."

"Thanks," I said.

Enthusiasm was cheap. It was nice to know that one's work was appreciated, but the best form of appreciation was financial.

"You have a real flair for this kind of thing," Jeff continued. "You really got under the skin of this model, this Karina."

That wasn't very surprising, because there was no Karina. I'd made her up. I was best at writing fiction, and most of what I'd written for Jeff had been a total fabrication. I had, however, used my own experiences modelling for Angela to add all the touches of verisimilitude.

"I'm glad you think so," I said.

"I've also got some photos through from the photographer you interviewed. Some were far too explicit for the magazine, but others were excellent. Just the kind of subtle erotic stuff I need to illustrate your article – which will be in the launch issue of the magazine."

"Good," I said, but I couldn't help wonder whether Angela and Dawn had thought it amusing to provide Jeff with nude photos of me. "By the way, were those the pictures of the blonde and the exercise bike?"

"No. Why?"

"Nothing. It was something Angela mentioned, that's all."

"A blonde and an exercise bike? Sounds interesting! Anyway, the other reason I'm phoning is to ask if you have any ideas for more articles?"

"Yes," I told him.

I was a writer. I might not have had anything else, but I had plenty of ideas.

TEN

At first I couldn't work out why Dawn looked so different, but then I realised – she had clothes on. Not that she was wearing very much, she was barefoot, dressed in just a short skirt and a skimpy vest.

She had phoned two hours ago, inviting me to the studio to see my photographs. I wasn't sure whether I wanted to see them, and neither was I sure whether I wanted to see Angela and Dawn again. What we did together had been great fun, but it was over. I didn't want to get involved. But I never wanted to get involved – and that was my problem, I knew.

"Angie will be out," Dawn had said.

I wondered if that was the only reason I was being asked, but I must have sounded hesitant, because Dawn added, "Don't worry, I won't try to seduce you again."

I laughed and replied, "Then it isn't worth me coming around, is it?"

But I went.

"Hi," she said.

"Hi," I said.

We looked at each other for a few seconds, then we both smiled, each remembering what had happened the first time I'd been there.

"Cup of tea?"

"Please."

"Angie had to go out, so I thought I'd give you a call."

I couldn't even remember leaving my phone number.

"She had to go and see some editor called Joe or Jim," Dawn continued, leading me into the kitchen.

"Jeff?" I said.

"That's the one. You know him?"

"It's because of him I came here. He's the one I wrote the article for."

"Ah, yes. Angie had me mail him a selection of photos. You never did interview me, did you?"

"It kind of slipped my mind. I think I was distracted."

Jeff must have asked Angela out for lunch, and I had my second such appointment with him the following week. I wondered how he was making out with her. Whatever his ultimate intentions, he would never get very far with Angela. Or with me . . .

"While Angie was away, I wondered what I should do," said Dawn, as she began making the tea. "Go find a couple of burly guys from a building site, bring them back here so they could fuck my brains out? Not again, I thought."

This was very similar to my raunchy daydream involving the two scaffolders. Perhaps such a scenario was a frequent female fantasy. Maybe there was a story there, an article on female sexual desires.

I already had a couple of ideas for what I could write next. One was inspired by Marvin, the stripping waiter at Stephanie's birthday lunch. Jeff wouldn't be interested in a feature on male strippers, of course, but I could write about the female equivalent. Not the kind of nude dancers found in clubs and bars, but those who worked as stripagrams. It was the incongruity which was so intriguing, that a girl would undress in an office or a factory.

It would make a good feature, and I wondered how I could go about it. For the piece on nude modelling I'd become a nude model, but I didn't really want to make a habit of such thorough research . . .

And I remembered when Don had phoned, the time that he discovered I was naked while talking to him. I could do an article on telephone sex lines. There were so many of them advertised in the back of the men's magazines. Most were recorded messages, but other lines claimed to be answered by "a real live girl" and promised such delights as "pussy talk: uncensored adult conversations with the hottest lips in town".

But Dawn was still speaking. "Then I remembered you hadn't seen your portfolio, the eight by ten glossies of your glossy cunt."

"You mean there really was a film in the camera?" I asked.

"More than one film," she replied. "A lot more. And the camera never lies. Well, hardly ever."

"How much do I have to pay to destroy the negatives?"

I said it as a joke, but I was half serious.

"I don't want your money," said Dawn, with a smile. She was also joking, but her smile could also mean she might want something else. "Sit down. You'll probably need to."

The kitchen was as almost as big as my flat, and I sat on one of the chairs at the glass-topped table. Dawn left the room, and when she came back she was carrying a big box of slides and a viewing machine. She plugged in the machine.

"Help yourself," she said, gesturing towards the trans-parencies.

I had very mixed feelings. Remembering what I'd done, I felt embarrassed, but I was also very curious to see the end result of all my efforts. The pictures existed, I couldn't deny them. And if they were there, I might as well see them.

Resting my hand on the viewer, I felt the electrical vibrations humming through its casing. I was never any good with mechanical devices. I couldn't drive, and even a toaster seemed an incredibly complex piece of machinery.

"How," I said, "how does this work?"

Dawn showed me how to use it, where to insert the slides. I picked one at random, bent my head over the eyepiece. I was amazed by the magnification, the clarity. There was nothing I hadn't seen before in any of the skin magazines I'd studied so assiduously. The only difference was that the photograph was of me . . .

I knew it was me, because it had been me who had bent backwards over the bicycle, thrusting my crotch into the air. My blonde crotch. From that kind of angle it could have been anyone. So I chose another slide, and another and another. Maybe it was true what Dawn had said, that no one really looked at a glamour model's face; the face was always on the periphery. But when I did see my face, I recognised myself – just about.

Those were my tits on view; my bare bum jutting out; my cunt open to view.

The next one I selected wasn't just of me. Dawn was also included, one of her hands on my breast, the other across my twat. The memories returned, and suddenly I was very warm again. My nipples dilated, and I could feel myself becoming moist. I switched off the machine.

"Milk but no sugar, wasn't it?" said Dawn. "If you want any of those, help yourself."

"Yes," I said, answering her question. "And no. They aren't really the kind of thing to hang on the wall."

"But wouldn't you like to look back on them when you're old and grey? When you're a granny, complaining about the

153

behaviour of the young 'uns, you could remember what a crazy vixen you used to be half a century ago!"

"Thanks," I said, as she gave me a mug of tea. Angela was away, so we didn't have the china tea set. "Is that what you plan to do? When your grandchildren ask what it used to be like in the old days, you'll show them nude pictures of yourself?"

Dawn laughed at the idea.

I said, "About these . . ."

"Take the lot," said Dawn, knowing exactly what I meant. "They're only photos. If it was me, I wouldn't care. But you're not a model, and so you'll keep wondering about them."

That was true, it had been in the back of my mind ever since leaving the studio. Although I had no regrets, these were a permanent record of my indiscretion.

"Burn them or bury them, have them enlarged, do what you want." Dawn slid the box of transparencies nearer, next to my drink.

"Are you sure? What about Angela?"

"She's got thousands of photographs, she won't miss a few. I can tell her I fucked up when I was developing them. Forget it, they're yours.

"Thanks," I said, and I rested my hand on the box.

I felt very relieved. There was no way I would keep the pictures, or at least not for long; but now that they were mine, I could spend time studying them before they were finally destroyed.

"What about the ones with you in?" I asked.

"I've plenty of me," Dawn replied, as she sipped her tea. "It's a pity there aren't any pictures of the three of us. Angie should have positioned a tripod and set the timer. I suppose she became too excited by what we were doing and couldn't wait to join us. I told you she gives great head. Wasn't I right?"

I nodded, not really sure what to say. I drank some tea while I thought of a reply. "You're not so bad yourself – or at least I *think* it was you . . ."

"This was me," said Dawn, and she thrust out her tongue. "And for a beginner, you showed a lot of potential. It makes a change from sucking cock, doesn't it?"

"There's also less to swallow, I suppose."

Dawn had her mug raised to her lips, and she laughed, the tea dribbling from her mouth and over her chin.

"Or you can do that," I said – and Dawn laughed even more. "It's the modern girl's dilemma," I added. "Spit or swallow?"

Dawn put her tea down, wiping her face with the back of her hand. "I think it's always best to swallow. If the head of the cock is far enough in, the sperm goes straight down your throat and you don't even have to taste it. You know what it's like otherwise – all that sticky stuff over your fingers or your clothes or your bed."

"Yes," I agreed, as if I were as experienced as her.

"I remember the first guy to stick his tongue up inside me," said Dawn, and she shook her head at the memory. "He hadn't a fucking clue what he should have been doing, you know."

"I know," I said, and I did.

Because of what had occurred between us, I felt as close to Dawn as any other girl I'd ever known. Cock-sucking and cunt-licking were things I'd never previously discussed, even with the guys involved. Especially with the guys involved. It was something to be done, not talked about. Without talking, however, there was no way of knowing if I'd done it right –

155

although perhaps there was no wrong way of giving a blowjob.

"You can do anything to a prick and it makes no difference," I continued. "An erect penis is so blatant it will come even if you rub it with sandpaper. But men don't realise that a cunt is infinitely more delicate and subtle."

"Right!" agreed Dawn. "It's just like them giving us the finger treatment. They think it's what we want, because it's what they want."

I crossed my legs without realising what I was doing.

"See what I mean!" she said. "Fingers straight in, rub-a-dub-dub. At least a tongue is wet, even if it doesn't know what it's supposed to be doing. They've got their heads between your legs, you would have thought they'd be able to see, wouldn't you?" She shook her head.

I was thinking about the first time I'd had a man's face between my thighs. His name was Peter, and it was during my first year at college. We'd gone out together, stayed in together, masturbated each other, until the time when he'd suddenly slid down, spread my legs and begun lapping at my cunt. He didn't do it very well; but because it had never happened to me before, I came almost immediately. And Peter assumed that almost immediately he could slide his cock into my mouth. All he got was a kiss on the tip of his knob, which was enough to make him ejaculate. I managed to avoid a face full of spunk by aiming his prick over my shoulder.

"What are you thinking about?" Dawn asked.

"Nothing," I said.

"So why are you smiling?"

I shook my head, and I smiled even more.

"Cock," said Dawn.

"What?"

"That's what you're thinking about: cock. Don't pretend you aren't! Tell me."

She was right, of course. I was thinking about cock, the first one I'd ever sucked. But I shook my head again.

"Tell me about yours and I'll tell you about mine," said Dawn.

I couldn't believe that I was going to say what I did, but I couldn't stop myself. I didn't even have the excuse of being drunk. The only explanation was that no one had ever asked me before, and maybe it was always something I'd wanted to talk about.

"Well," I said, and I drained my tea.

"Well?" prompted Dawn, giving me an immediate refill.

"His name was Sam," I said. I spoke slowly, remembering. "I met him when I was at college. I did literature. Sam was a poet. He'd had a few volumes of his own work published, and he gave readings all over the country, but to make a living he lectured at the university one term a year. He was the way you imagine a poet should be, wild, romantic, unkempt, handsome. And a total bastard. Every girl on the course fell for him, and he went through them all. All except me."

"You played hard to get?" said Dawn. "I never did. I was always too easy."

"I didn't deliberately play hard to get, not at first. I suppose I was just harder than all the others. Once he'd fucked all of them, it was my turn. I was a challenge to him. How could I possibly resist his charismatic personality? But the more he chased me, the more I avoided him. Whenever he asked me out, I was always busy. He started sending me poems, everything from romantic sonnets to obscene limericks. So in the end . . ." I shrugged.

157

"I know," said Dawn. "It's all in the pheromones. What happened?"

"Once I went out with him, I wondered why I'd resisted for so long. He could be so charming and knew exactly how to flatter me, where to take me. Not out to eat or for a drink, nothing so mundane. We'd go for long moonlit walks and talk about how to set everything right with the world. He did most of the talking. Being a poet, he really knew how to use the language – and maybe that was why he was so good with his tongue."

Dawn smiled. She was a good listener, encouraging me to say what I'd never said before.

"We'd gone out into the country to watch the sun come up on mid-summer morning, and then we went swimming in a lake. It was so icy cold that we hugged each other to get warm. The hugging led to kissing, and then Sam started stroking my body. We fell onto the grass, and he was licking my tits and fingering my slit. Then he went down on me. And he was wonderful, wonderful. He knew exactly what he was doing, probably because he'd done it so often, having licked so many other cunts before mine. It was the ultimate, the absolute best. He used his lips, his tongue, his fingers, his beard, maybe even his nose. But my clit had never been so well treated. You know what it's like when you just come and come, and each time it gets better and better?"

Dawn nodded, sighing. "I know."

"He'd given me so much, and I knew I had to do the same for him. I lay back recovering, stroking his prick, probably hoping I could get away with just wanking him off. He had his hand on the back of my neck, applying light pressure, and at the same time he was sliding closer, bringing his cock nearer and nearer my mouth. I couldn't pretend I didn't know what he wanted, so I bent my head and I gave the end of his knob a quick lick. It became addictive. My hand was around the shaft, and I flicked my tongue across the dome several times. I ran the tip of my tongue around the ridge – and suddenly I'd sucked the glans into my mouth."

I was watching Dawn while I spoke. Her mouth was open and her tongue out. She was unconsciously acting out what I was saying, almost as if she were following precise instructions.

"Having done that, I drew more and more of the flesh between my lips. It was like a test, trying to find how much cock I could get into my mouth, but it kept slipping back. I didn't realise what was happening at first, because I thought I was controlling the situation, like Sam had done with my cunt. But he was in total command of his prick, not me. I was licking the shaft inside with my tongue, rubbing it outside with my fingers; but he was gliding it in and out of my mouth. He was fucking my face . . ."

I took a mouthful of tea, holding it on my tongue before swallowing it down. And I remembered how Sam's spunk had filled my mouth and coated my tongue. I'd managed to swallow that down, too.

"Did you enjoy it?" asked Dawn.

"Yes," I said truthfully, "I did."

"It's odd, isn't? When you think of the idea it seems repulsive; but when you're actually blowing a guy, it feels great. You do it because you know they adore being sucked off, but you also get a lot of pleasure from it. Even getting a mouthful of come isn't too bad."

I nodded. Sam the poet had filled my throat with his hot creamy seed, and I never saw him again.

"What about you?" I asked.

159

"What?" Dawn frowned. "Maybe we should go and find a couple of building workers after all . . ."

"You said you'd tell your story if I told mine," I reminded her.

"I lied," she said.

"I'll be back in a minute," said Dawn, and she left the room.

She had taken me into the lounge. The walls were covered with contemporary paintings, which made me realise I'd seen no photographs on display anywhere in the apartment or studio. When Dawn returned, she was carrying a video cassette. She took it from the case, and slipped it into the machine. Then she drew the velvet curtains, blocking out all the sunlight which had flooded the room.

"What's this?" I asked, picking up the discarded video case. It was a children's cartoon.

There was a huge screen on the wall above the video, the television, the stereo, all the various other electronic equipment, and the picture became visible as the room darkened.

"It isn't quite what you asked me," said Dawn, "but near enough. Sit down."

She sat on the floor, on one of the embroidered Oriental carpets, and leaned back against the padded sofa. I did the same, leaning against one of the chairs, and I looked up at the screen.

Zany music blared from the two huge speakers on the opposite corners. Dawn used the remote to reduce the volume. The credits came up. There was something odd about them, but I wasn't really paying attention because I'd glanced at Dawn, wondering what was going on. She was staring intently at the wall screen, trying not to smile.

A cartoon dinosaur started chasing a tiny cartoon

caveman across the screen. The man evaded the creature's lunge and yelled something which I couldn't understand. Then I realised why the credits had seemed so strange; they had been in a foreign language.

"You should be watching," Dawn told me. "You might think this is the best part."

"If this is the best . . ."

"Okay, okay, fast forward."

She pressed a button. The tyrannosaur raced even faster, then plunged over the edge of a cliff, while the caveman drifted down by parachute. The next scene showed the dinosaur roasting over a volcano, on a spit being turned by a tiny man wearing a chef's hat and a furry loincloth.

Then suddenly the cartoon figure was replaced by the image of a twentieth-century man, full-size and wearing cowboy hat. That was all, just a hat. His back was to the camera; his back and his bare behind. He was very hairy, I noticed; perhaps modern man was not so very different from those who had lived in caves. The film slowed to normal speed, and the music changed to bland synthesised rock.

"Home movies?" I asked.

"Kind of," said Dawn. "It's a movie you can watch at home."

I was still holding the tape box, and I glanced at the cover again: a pterodactyl ridden by a caveman wearing a flying helmet.

"Camouflage," explained Dawn – which could only mean that she kept the true contents of the cassette hidden from Angela.

The camera moved closer to the naked cowboy, who was simply standing in the middle of an ordinary room. His arms were in front of him, hidden from view. But they came into sight as the camera moved around. He was stroking the hair of the girl who had been hidden from view. Her hair was jet black, shorter than it now was. She was on her knees, with the cowboy's cock in her mouth. It was Dawn, of course.

"I thought I'd show you instead of tell you," she said. "Although I admit this wasn't the first time I licked a dick."

I said nothing. I watched the screen in amazement. I knew this kind of movie existed, but I'd never seen one. I'd never even seen a photo of cock-sucking. I'd performed such an act myself, but to actually watch it happen on a screen, far larger than life, and to have the girl who was doing it sitting next to me . . .

I watched as Dawn's head slowly bobbed up and down, the cowboy's fat prick sliding in and out of her mouth. She wasn't using her hands, perhaps because they would have obscured the view. The camera moved even closer, filling the screen with her face and the wet cock she was licking and sucking with such undisguised relish.

As well as the music, I could hear slurping noises, the sounds of heavy male panting, and then, "Oh, baby, that's so good, so good. Take it all down, babe. Swallow me good. You're the best, baby . . ."

Dawn turned the sound off.

"Great dialogue, huh?" she said. "I couldn't say anything because my mouth was full."

I glanced away from the screen for a moment. In the gloom I noticed Dawn was grinning as she watched herself greedily sucking on the man's prick. Her screen self leaned back, letting the thick tool glide from her mouth. It was more than thick, it was also very long, and she wiped the saliva-coated head all around her mouth as if it were lipstick. She gazed up adoringly, her tongue running down the length of the shaft and back. Then she licked all around the gleaming glans before sliding the flesh back into her mouth.

There was still nothing for me to say; Dawn wasn't showing me this so that I'd congratulate her on her acting skills. But the more I watched, the warmer I became.

On screen, she drew her head back quickly, and her tongue was shiny with spunk. He had come in her mouth, but then he ejaculated again, and a fountain of spunk splashed against Dawn's cheek. She directed his cock towards her other cheek, and another spurt of sperm splattered onto her skin. He came again, and again, all over her face.

Her mouth was open wide as if in passion, and she ran her tongue across the tip of the glans, lapping up the last drops of semen. As she leaned back, for a brief moment there was a thin thread of spunk between her lips and the cowboy's cock.

Dawn froze the picture. On screen, her face was speckled with semen; her eyes were closed and she smiled in triumph. Off screen, she pressed another button – and on screen, streamers of come leapt from her face, flying through the air and straight into the cowboys's knob.

I laughed because it looked so silly when shown in reverse. Another button, and a shot of sperm slowly arced from the glans towards Dawn's cheek. She was running the video in slow motion, and I laughed again.

"If only it happened that slow in real life," she said, "think how much less washing we'd have to do."

There were several things I wanted to say, several questions I had to ask. I was very intrigued by what I'd seen, but I didn't know where to begin.

Dawn stopped the tape again, catching a streak of silver in mid-flight before it could hit her face.

163

"I think they should show these in schools," she said. "Kids would learn a hell of a lot more from a porn vid than from any sex education class."

She pressed another button. The film ran on, and she was sucking someone else off. He was horizontal, she was underneath in the back of a car, but otherwise it wasn't much different. Like the cowboy, he ejaculated over her, although across her breasts instead of her face.

"I suppose that's to prove you're not pretending," I said, speaking for the first time in several minutes.

"That's right," agreed Dawn. "The man has always to shoot his stuff for the camera. A come shot, as it's known in the trade. A good long squirt, none of that dribbly stuff."

And then on screen her image was fellating yet another hard cock.

"Not much of a plot, is there?" I said.

She laughed. "These are edited highlights. Just like football matches when they only show the goals. Dawn's greatest sucks, you could say. I'll find something else." She flicked a button and the image blanked.

I gazed at the empty screen, thinking.

A minute later, it was no longer empty and there was something else to watch and think about. No massive prick thrust between Dawn's full lips this time, but instead two naked girls writhed on a bed in the sixty-nine position.

One of them was Dawn, of course, and for a few seconds I suspected that the other was Angela. But when I saw her face in close-up, her tongue lapping at Dawn's pink cunt, I realised she was someone else. The unknown girl's face filled the screen until the camera zoomed in on her tongue, on Dawn's twat, every detail magnified by the lens.

"Wow," I muttered in utter astonishment, as Dawn's

164

swollen labia flooded with her inner juices and she achieved on-screen orgasm.

"And that's to show I'm not pretending," she whispered in my ear.

I'd been so involved with the video I hadn't noticed her moving closer to me, but now she was by my side, and her arm went around my shoulder, pulling me even nearer. I turned my head to hers and we kissed, but from the corner of my eye I was still watching the wall screen.

While our tongues intertwined, she fondled my breasts. I put my hand on her thigh and slid my fingers up beneath her skirt. She wasn't wearing any underwear, which meant it only took a few seconds until she was naked. It took only slightly longer for me to strip off.

"Another lie," said Dawn, as she skinned my knickers down. "I said I wouldn't seduce you."

"Shut up and fuck me," I said, and I silenced myself by filling my mouth with her left tit.

Then we were rolling around on the floor together. The video was still running, and at first we took that as our cue, doing to each other exactly what was happening on the tape. They kissed and we kissed. Dawn licked her screen partner's left nipple, and I did it to her. Dawn began tonguing the other girl's twat, and so my hungry mouth descended upon Dawn's tasty cunt, my tongue caressing her clit.

And when she did the same to me, every one of my senses was wiped out by sexual overloaded. I became oblivious to everything except for the absolute passion and the ultimate ecstasy of the intimate sensual delights which I was sharing.

ELEVEN

"Dawn, darling!"

The man embraced her, pulling her close and kissing her. They kissed for a long time, then finally their lips parted, but they kept on holding hands.

We were on a movie set, or more accurately a video set – or even more accurately inside a country mansion where a video film was being made. It was the kind of film I had seen the previous week when I was with Dawn. Not that I'd seen very much of it. But as soon as Dawn had started her on-screen fellatio, I'd realised that a feature on porn movies would be ideal for Jeff and his magazine.

Dawn introduced me and then said, "This is Murphy."

He was dressed in denim: jeans, shirt, waistcoat, cap. The jeans were tucked into cowboy boots, his long grey hair hung from beneath the cap. Murphy was tall and lean, unshaven and smiling. He could have been any age between thirty and fifty.

"Any friend of Dawn's," he said, "is very lucky . . . !"

He let go of Dawn's hand and shook mine, politely. His other arm was still around Dawn, and he began massaging her bra-less boobs. She slapped his hand away.

"Dawn could have been a star, you know," he said to me, rubbing at the hand which she had slapped. "She was my super nova, a star to have eclipsed every constellation in the galaxy, a pulsar who sent my pulse rate into galactic overdrive."

"Throw a bucket of water over him, please," said Dawn.

"Her lips, her tits, her hair, her flesh, her cunt," proclaimed Murphy, gesturing to the various parts of Dawn's anatomy as he spoke. "Oh, Dawn, Dawn! Come back, all is forgiven."

"You see how he could talk a girl into anything?" Dawn said to me.

"But she," Murphy countered, "talked me into allowing you here."

It hadn't taken too much to persuade Dawn to contact Murphy. I'd simply drawn my mouth away from her hot twat and asked if I could meet the person who had made the films which were up on the wall behind us.

"Yes," she'd replied. "Yes, yes, yes!"

Organising our visit had taken a while, because Dawn first had to locate Murphy. That seemed to be his only name. It had been a few years since she'd worked for him and she wasn't even sure whether he was still making porn movies. But he was. Dawn had to wait until Angela was away for a couple of days so we could make our visit. Until then, I hadn't realised how jealous Angela was, that she wanted to know what Dawn was doing every hour of the day. And so, at every opportunity, Dawn did whatever she could . . .

Hence our drive into the country. I hired the car, on Jeff's promised expenses, and Dawn drove.

"It's very good of you to let me . . ." I paused, trying hard not to use the word "come".

"That's okay," said Murphy. "If you want to write about porn films, write about the best. Mine." Taking Dawn's hand again, he led us up the broad flight of marble stairs.

"Quite a place, huh?" He pointed with his free hand. "Tapestries hung from the walls, crystal chandeliers hung from the ceilings. But if you want to see something really well-hung . . ."

"I forgot he was this bad," Dawn told me.

We went up onto the landing and into a panelled galley which was lined with old paintings. I took no notice of the paintings at first until I saw that Dawn was studying them very intently. Then I realised they were pornographic pictures from the eighteenth century. The men and women were wearing period costumes, more or less, but that didn't stop them from sucking and screwing. Masters would be fucking the maids, taking them from the rear as they lit the fire; or it wouldn't be the table which was laid, but the serving girls; or the cook would be tasting the aristocrat's dick instead of the stew.

It was always the lord of the house who was taking his pleasure with a member of the lower orders. There were no illustrations of an upper class lady being serviced by a blacksmith or going down on the butler.

"Great stuff," commented Murphy. "And there's going to be plenty of great stuffing going on in front of these pictures! You go ahead, I'll be with you in a minute."

The hall was full of lights, cameras, audio equipment and plenty of people, some of whom were naked. There were three nude girls, and one guy. He was sitting in an ancient armchair, reading a book and seemingly oblivious to everything going on around him.

Two of the girls were rolling about together on the carpet, kissing and stroking, licking each other's tits and caressing one another's buttocks. Their lack of enthusiasm was obvious, but this didn't seem to bother the group of men who were watching. Some of them had cameras, lightweight video recorders as well as ordinary 35mm cameras, and were busy filming and clicking away.

A man in a business suit stood up against the wall, and the

third nude girl was on her knees in front of him, trying to unzip his pants. He was endeavouring to avoid the blonde's attention.

"No, don't," he protested.

"Don't you want me to?" she asked.

"No, thank you."

"But I want to." She laughed, wrapping her other arm around the man's legs to prevent him escaping.

"Please don't do that," he told her.

Another man stood nearby, his camera aimed on the blonde and her reluctant companion.

"Smile, Henry," he said.

"Put that fucking camera away!" yelled the man, and he covered his face with his arms.

That gave the girl the opportunity to work unhampered on Henry's pants, and she soon had them down around his knees.

"'Click!'

"Lick his dick, baby," said the man with the camera. "You can give your wife the picture, Henry. Then maybe she'll find out how to suck cock."

But the girl simply laughed again, and she stood up. I gazed at her in amazement. She was blonde, but between her legs she was completely shaven. The man with the camera aimed at her crotch, and there was a series of 'clicks'.

The girl suddenly noticed Dawn and me, and she halted. She put her hands on her hips, watching us. She didn't seem too pleased that we were there. I tore my gaze away from the blonde's totally bare twat and nodded to the man who was fastening his pants.

"Who are they all?" I asked Dawn.

"Murphy used to call them 'investors'," she said. "If

anyone put up a thousand, he'd let them watch for a while. That was all they ever got for their money. He'd put on a show, then get rid of them and start the real work. And I suppose whoever owns this place is also here. That's how Murphy pays for his locations. I wonder who it is this time? He must be worth a lot to have a place like this."

"If he's worth that much, why would he allow a film to be made here?"

"Because everyone's a voyeur," replied Dawn. "He wants to watch the fucky-sucky." She looked around, as if trying to see who might own the mansion where we'd found ourselves.

I wondered if the same applied to me. Was I a voyeur? Was that why I was really here, to watch the fucking and the sucking? Perhaps it was.

"Sometimes location fees are paid by giving the owner a guest role," added Dawn. "You can guess what sort of role."

"Yes," I said.

"But it usually ends up on the cutting-room floor. Some of them can't even get a hard-on in front of a camera. It takes a professional to fuck on screen. Male or female."

Dawn was staring at the blonde as she spoke, who could overhear what was being said. Suddenly her eyes widened with recognition and she relaxed.

"I've retired," Dawn told her. "I'm not here to take your job. I'm Dawn."

"I'm Liz," said the girl, who then looked at me.

I shook my head, making it clear that I was in a different line of work. Dawn and Liz moved towards each other and began talking. I glanced around again. Everything seemed totally disorganised, but that was nothing compared to what happened when Murphy arrived on the scene.

"Clear the set," he ordered. "Clear the set!"

He screamed and he yelled, he swore and grew angry, his face became red and he began grabbing at the men who had been watching the two girls, and he shoved them towards the exit. Then Murphy caught sight of me, strode across, and I thought I was also going to be thrown out. Instead he smiled.

"Bastards," he said, his voice already calm, his complexion returning to normal. "What do they expect? They've had their money's worth; they've seen the rehearsals."

"Rehearsals?" said Dawn, as she joined us. "How do you rehearse a come shot? Your studs must have changed since my day, Murph."

He gestured dismissively. "I'll send them all a tape when it's finished. Maybe. Okay, let's get the show on the road!" He gazed around the room, then nodded. "First there was chaos," he said, "and then there was creation."

He spun around, giving more orders, bullying and threatening.

"He's wasted here," Dawn said to me. "He's directed commercials, done television plays, so why does he still do this? I got out of it, although I suppose I didn't get far. I was never going to be an actress, but Murphy . . ." She shook her head. "I suppose it's because he likes it."

We waited. I'd heard that the majority of filming was waiting, and it was true.

And finally I stood and watched while Murphy filmed part of his movie. Erotic or pornographic, that was a matter of semantics.

In the greater scheme of things, it was all so trivial. Sex was a celebration of life; the true obscenities in our world were war and corruption, brutality and famine.

But enough of philosophy—

—back to the fucking.

The naked guy put down his book and stood up. He was like some Greek god, lithe and muscular; although perhaps the ancient gods didn't have mermaids tattooed on their forearms. He'd been reading Tolstoy, I noticed. In the original Russian.

Even in the non-functional position his knob was very impressive, although Murphy didn't seem very impressed.

"Get it up, Bob," he said.

"I'll do it," said one of the girls who had been writhing on the floor a few minutes earlier. They were both slim brunettes, and both still had their pubic hair.

The girl took hold of Bob's penis. It looked massive in her small hand as she began to stroke it between her fingers; and it quickly became even more massive. It began to grow, responding to her expert touch, and was soon hard.

I watched in fascination, never having seen another girl do this to a man. I was even more fascinated when she went down on him. She knelt in front of Bob, licking the length of his stiff prick, then engulfing the swollen glans between her lips. She had to stretch her mouth to accommodate the girth.

My heartbeat increased and I began to sweat, and I felt my cunt grow moist. I glanced away for a moment, and I realised no one else was watching the girl's oral endeavours. Everyone was busy with something else, even Dawn; she was in the corner, still talking to Liz. It was as if this scene was being played out exclusively for me, that the brunette was sucking on Bob's hard knob simply for my benefit. I noticed that Bob was watching me, and I blushed.

"That's enough," he said. He drew his erection free of the girl's mouth. He kept watching me, but I was watching his cock: it was wet with saliva and streaked with pink from the girl's lipstick.

"You can have another taste later," he said, and he was talking to me, not the girl.

I managed to turn away, and I went over to the other side of the room in order to catch my breath.

Murphy's idea was to film a number of sequences, each of which matched up with the erotic paintings which hung in the gallery. Bob and the other girl who had gone through the lesbian charade were to be filmed in front of the painting of a country gentleman fucking a milkmaid, and they positioned themselves accordingly. There were only six in the film crew, including Murphy, but the couple seemed to be surrounded by lights, cameras, microphones.

Feeling cooler and less aroused, and not wanting to miss anything, I pushed myself forward once more. It seemed some filming had already occurred, that the pair had started off wearing similar clothing to the two in the painting. During this sequence they had stripped off, and gone through a few preliminary sexual gymnastics. This, as well as what I'd witnessed earlier, was what Murphy claimed was enough to satisfy all the hangers-on.

"Let's go," he said. "Lights, sound, camera, fuck . . ."

And that was what happened. The guy started fucking the girl, just doing it up against the wall, up against the picture. It was what I'd expected, but expectation wasn't sufficient to dull my amazement. To actually watch it happening a few yards away from me, to see a real cock slide into a real cunt caused my pulse to race again, my sweat to flow once more.

Murphy kept telling them what to do, exactly as Angela had given me orders when I'd been posing for her. But he had two of them to command, and he was also directing the cameramen. There were two cameras focusing on what was happening, one going in close for the intimate details, the other collating the overall picture.

"That's good, that's good," said Murphy. "Turn around, darling, take it from the rear."

The girl had been pinned to the wall while Bob slid his knob deep into her twat, his powerful strokes lifting her feet from the ground. Now he withdrew and obediently she turned around, bending over and spreading her legs to be shafted from behind. Bob resumed pumping into her.

"Not much longer, Murph," he said.

That was the first time either of them had spoken, and I wondered why it was worth recording any of the sound. The only things picked up would have been Murphy's orders: "Faster. Pull it out more so we can see it. Slower. Cup her breasts. Stroke his balls. Lean back and sigh."

Now Murphy said, "Slide it out. This way, darling. Take it in your mouth."

The girl obeyed, turning around and going down on her knees as she sucked on the solid male flesh.

"Hair out of your face," Murphy told her.

She tucked her hair behind her ear to give a better view of the shaft which was slipping in and out of her lips.

"Here we go," said Bob, and he withdrew his tool from the girl's mouth.

"Look happy," Murphy told the girl.

A moment later her face was splattered with spurts of spunk.

Dawn was standing next to me, although I wasn't aware of her until she spoke. I was too mesmerised by what I was watching.

"Don't call us, we'll call you," she muttered, shaking her head at the girl's performance.

"It's the girls who make any film," said Dawn. "Think of all the famous names, and how many men are there compared to the girls?"

I shrugged. I didn't even know there were any famous names.

"Porn films are made for men," Dawn continued, "so it's the girls the viewers are interested in, not the studs. The thrusting cock belongs to all the guys watching. It's they who are doing the fucking, who are being sucked off. Even female erotica, the kind of porn made for women, is watched by more men than women."

I shrugged again. I didn't even know there were any porn films for women.

"Female porn?" I asked. "How's that any different?"

"More cunt licking than cock sucking. A higher ratio of males. Not so phallocentric."

It was half an hour later, and we were drinking coffee while Murphy set up another scene. The other three girls were sitting away from us, and they kept looking in our direction. Bob was recovering his virility, drinking tea and reading Tolstoy.

"He can get it up again very soon," said Dawn, "because that's his job. But he won't be able to shoot as much spunk for quite a while. That's why the girls make any film. In movies, as in real life, we're the insatiable ones. We can have multiple climaxes. They can't."

"But they can pretend," I said.

"We can. They can't. Like I said, they have to ejaculate for real, whip it out for the camera and spurt over faces and

175

hair, tits and bums. They need the girls to make them look good, and it's the girls who do all the work. We're the ones in close-up, sucking dick, swallowing spunk."

"'We?' I thought you'd retired?"

Dawn laughed, then shook her head, glancing over to the other three girls. "That was about the worst blowjob I've ever seen. She didn't do anything."

"What should she have done?" I asked. "She made him come."

And watching the slim brunette suck Bob's prick had almost been enough to make me come, too.

"It would have been more of an achievement not to," said Dawn, "to have made the scene last longer by teasing him and his knob. Drawing it in and out, flicking her tongue across the dome, circling it around the ridge behind the head. And when he climaxed, she wasted the opportunity. She could have done so much in those few seconds." She shook her head again and sipped at her coffee.

Like glamour photography, there was far more to making erotic movies than I'd ever guessed. "What?" I prompted.

"She had to love that cock, to worship it, to kiss it and lick it as though it was the most wonderful thing in her life. When that guy ejaculated, she just let it happen, as though it was nothing to do with her. He came because of her, but the way it looked he came in spite of her."

The girl's reaction had seemed fine to me, but I was no expert.

"She should have aimed his cock into her mouth," Dawn continued, "let him spray over her lips so that she could have licked at the drops of spunk afterwards. She should have moaned as if she was also having an orgasm, that her mouth functioned like her cunt. She should have leaned closer at the end, lapping up the final creamy drops with the tip of her tongue."

"And I remember your tongue . . ."

Dawn and I both turned at the sound of the voice, staring up at the man who had silently walked up behind us.

"Hello, Dawn," he said, and he smiled.

Dawn gazed and him in wide-eyed astonishment. "Phil?" she said. "Phil!"

She jumped to her feet, knocking her chair over, and she embraced the newcomer. He lifted her up and spun her around. Phil was in his mid-thirties, with amazing blue eyes.

"This is Phil," Dawn told me, once he had put her down. "My favourite fuck!" She couldn't stop smiling.

"Wish I could say the same about Dawn," said Phil, and he winked at me.

Dawn made as if to punch him in the crotch, but she laughed. "What are you doing here?"

"I invited him," said Murphy, as he joined us. "Thought we'd have a reunion."

"I'm not making any more fuck films," said Dawn.

"Who asked you to?" said Murphy. "But while Phil's here . . ."

"Some good looking young fillies you got there, Murph," said Phil. "Maybe I should meet 'em before I fuck 'em."

Murphy took Phil over to the three naked girls, and he also introduced Bob. The six of them sat down together to talk.

I noticed Dawn watching. "We can leave if you want," I offered.

"We'll stay," she said. "Murphy hopes to get me and Phil back together in front of the cameras – but he won't."

"Phil and Bob are dining together," said Murphy. "The girls

are serving them, but they become the meal. Lots of drilling and filling. Whatever three girls and two guys can do to each other, I want you to do it. Okay?"

We were in a different room, where there was a huge table. Phil and Bob sat at opposite ends, both dressed in period costume. Some of their clothing seemed anachronistic, but I imagined that was of little consequence. They wouldn't be wearing anything for very long, I supposed.

"Let's roll," said Murphy to his cast and crew. "Liz!"

The door opened and the blonde girl entered, carrying a crystal decanter and two wine glasses. As she poured Phil's wine, he slowly raised her long dress, lifting it higher and higher until her bare backside was revealed. With a flick of his wrist, Liz's dress was gone. She was naked to the waist, and Phil gazed at her shaven twat, then beckoned to Bob to share his discovery. Together, they removed the rest of Liz's clothing and lifted her onto the table. The camera moved in close on her hairless cunt.

All the time Murphy had been yelling instructions, telling them what to do and feeding them lines of dialogue. He also reached out and collected the cut crystal decanter and glasses before they could be smashed. Phil, I noticed, needed little instruction and could even improvise his own dialogue – not that there was very much, and almost all of it was anatomical.

Then the other two girls entered, saw what was going on, and began pulling at the men's clothes, who also tore at their garments. Before too long, all five of them were naked and fucking and sucking.

I'd never seen anything like it. Never imagined anything like it.

Whatever a cock could do to a part of the female anatomy,

178

Phil or Bob did with their rampant pricks. Whatever a female tongue could do to man or women, Liz and the other two girls did. Knobs slid into eager mouths and more eager twats. Tongues slipped into mouths and twats and around cocks, sometimes licking swollen tools as they glided into cunts. The two guys took one of the girls at either end, one cock in her mouth, another in her twat; while the other two girls devoted their attention to one another, each supping upon cunt juice. Then two of the girls concentrated on Bob, one licking his balls, the other his dick, while Bob's tongue was flicking in and out of the gaping twat of Liz, who was busy fellating Phil – who was fingering the clits of the first two girls.

Dawn had been dismissive of male capabilities, but I was very impressed at the staying power of both Phil and Bob. There was lots of moaning and sighing from the feminine trio on the table, but I guessed it was all faked.

Probably the only person in the room who really climaxed was me. My panties were sopping wet and I hadn't even touched myself. All I needed to do was watch; that was sufficient to bring me off.

The video crew seemed totally unaffected, as if they could have been filming anything. Perhaps they were used to this sort of thing and had become immune, although I found that difficult to believe. They shoved their camera lenses ever nearer, focusing on cocks in cunts and in mouths, lips sucking upon pink twat and purple glans.

"Oh, no," muttered Dawn, and I glanced around as she swiftly shed her clothes and joined the orgy of glistening naked bodies which rolled and writhed upon the table.

I saw Murphy smile. By now he was no longer shouting orders, because no one was listening any more.

I wasn't really surprised that Dawn had been unable to resist, because I was very tempted to strip off my own garments and join in the orgiastic fun. But I had far more inhibitions, and I had to content myself with just watching the heaving mass of intertwining flesh.

Liz had control of Phil's knob, which was halfway down her throat, but she became distracted when Dawn started licking at the swollen clit which protruded from her shaven twat. I felt a pang of jealousy. Dawn knew exactly what she was doing, her tongue and fingertips bringing Liz rapidly towards an ecstasy which could not have been faked. The blonde released Phil's penis, and instantly Dawn claimed it as her own, guiding it straight into her cunt as she mounted him. In the afterglow of her climax, Liz began stroking Dawn's tits, moving closer to her. They kissed, embracing tightly – and I grew even more envious.

Phil reached out for Liz, pulling her above him so he could tongue her twat. While he was fucking Dawn and sucking Liz, who were kissing each other, the two brunettes were locked together with Bob. They lay in a triangle at the other end of the table. As he fucked one in the mouth, he licked at the glistening twat of the other. That meant one girl's mouth was vacant, one girl's cunt was unoccupied, but they proved to be a perfect fit – and so they busied themselves with each other.

I was hotter and stickier than ever, and I held my thighs clenched together, wishing there was a spare tongue for my aching cunt.

"It's squirt time," announced Phil.

Dawn raised her hips, freeing his cock. Phil's shaft was shiny from her cunt and Liz's mouth, and it was time for the cameras to catch him in a spectacular ejaculation.

180

For a second everything become still, everyone waiting for Murphy to call the shot.

Murphy said, "Ah . . ."

And then I remembered the thought which had crossed my mind when Marvin had stripped in the Italian restaurant. I reached down and grabbed one of the wine glasses, handing it to Dawn.

"In this," I said.

Dawn held the glass towards Phil's cock, and a moment later his firm flesh trembled and erupted, surges of hot come gushing out. She caught every silvery spurt in the crystal, not losing a single drop.

Then she raised the glass above her mouth and tilted it as she leaned her head back. The warm spunk dripped down towards her parted lips. A moment later Liz's face was next to hers, sharing the exquisite liqueur. The thick drops rained down upon their parched lips and their thirsty tongues. What was left in the glass they scooped out with their fingers. Liz greedily sucked at Dawn's spunk-coated index finger, and Dawn hungrily lapped at the final drops from Liz's finger. And then their tongues roved across one another's faces, finding the stray spots of semen which speckled their cheeks.

The cut crystal glass which Dawn had discarded rolled towards the edge of the table and fell. Murphy caught the glass, examined it, then looked at me.

"Would you like to write a movie?" he asked. "Have you got any ideas?"

TWELVE

Afterwards, we went for a meal. I kept thinking of Don who had spent so much of his time attempting to sell a movie. And now, without even trying, I'd been asked to write one. It wasn't what you knew; it was who you knew. A porn film might not be in the same league as a major Hollywood production, but I thought I'd better not tell Don about it.

I probably wouldn't be able to tell him about anything, in fact. Since we last met, I'd phoned him every day; but I'd only talked to his answering machine. He never got back to me, and I was beginning to get concerned. Had he really carried out his absurd threat to find a "job"?

It seemed that Murphy's reunion between Dawn and Phil had been a great success, and not only because of what happened during today's filming. While the rest of the cast and crew had gone their own ways, the four of us went out together after the shooting was over – and the other two were inseparable.

After filming the orgy scene, I'd found a bathroom and taken a long cool shower, while Dawn and Phil had found a bedroom and continued to make up for lost time. I knew because I went through the wrong door, although after what I'd already witnessed it didn't really matter. Murphy and I had to wait ages until they were ready to leave the mansion.

"I've done so many of these films they've probably become too similar," said Murphy, as he poured me another glass of wine. He watched as I lifted it to my lips, and I knew he was remembering what I was remembering. We both glanced at Dawn and Phil, whose glasses were untouched. They were still talking as if there was no one else in the world except them, their voices low and intimate.

"Your idea of the glass was simply brilliant," Murphy continued. "So how about writing a whole movie? You don't have to worry too much about the dialogue or the mechanics of fucking."

"What else is there?" I asked, but I knew exactly what he meant. He just wanted basic plot lines, new ideas to get people out of their clothes and into bed together – into bed and anywhere else . . .

Murphy laughed, knowing that I knew. "What I need is characterisation, motivation, development. That's what makes the difference between a cheap fuck-flick and a good erotic movie. There are too many amateurs in the business these days, which gives everyone a bad name. Anyone with a camcorder thinks he can make a movie." He shook his head.

"What kind of film do you want?" I asked.

"That's up to you, although it's best to keep it contemporary. But whatever you want to do, how ever many people, how ever many combinations, I bet you can't produce something that's beyond our capabilities. If the human mind can think of it, the human body can do it."

"Sounds like a challenge," I said, wondering just what dirty deeds I could devise.

"If she writes it," said Dawn, her attention diverted from Phil for a few seconds, "I'll be in it."

Murphy nodded, and he smiled.

"That means me, too," added Phil.

Murphy nodded again, and he smiled even more.

I sipped at my wine. "What about . . . ?"

". . . the money?"

"Yes."

"It all depends on how many pages you produce. Say I want a one-hour film, we can divide that fifty-fifty between plot and fucking." He stared into his glass, tilting his head from side to side as he did the maths, then he named a figure.

I tried not to choke on my wine.

"Straight cash, of course," he said. "No cheques, no taxes – but no royalties, either."

"Er . . . sounds . . . er . . . fine," I said, and I drained my glass.

"And if you want," said Murphy, giving me another refill, "you can do a guest appearance in the movie."

Again, I knew exactly what he meant. "Like a stunt girl, you mean?"

"Well . . . it rhymes with stunt."

"Perhaps not," I said.

Murphy looked me up and down. "Pity," he said, then he reached into the bag he had been carrying. "Maybe these will help you." He piled half a dozen video cassettes on the table in front of me.

I picked up the first one, which showed a girl with two hard cocks stuffed into her mouth. The second pictured a girl's face being showered with spunk from the prick she held. If these were the covers, I wondered what happened during the rest of the films.

"I haven't got a video," I told him. I was only an impoverished author.

"But you've seen this kind of thing before?" said Murphy.

"Yes," I said, remembering the tape that Dawn had played for me – although I hadn't seen very much of it once I became distracted.

184

Murphy shrugged. "Seen one, seen 'em all. Perhaps it's best if you take a different approach. You're coming from outside the field, and I've been inside for too long. But together we can come up with something really new and different. Ah, let's eat."

The meal had arrived, and even Dawn and Phil found time to eat dinner. By now it was my attention which was distracted. My head was buzzing with ideas for the movie I was going to write.

I'd no idea how to go about writing a script, but Murphy said that didn't matter – he'd still no real idea how to make a film.

He started with a basic idea, then made everything up as he went along. "And sometimes it shows," he said. "All you have to do is get a few pages down on paper, then we can take it from there. But often the best ideas happen spontaneously, like your suggestion of the wine glass. You should be there during the filming, coming up with new ideas all the time."

I wasn't too sure about that, because I knew that Murphy would try and persuade me to join in. And, like Dawn, I might not be able to resist.

But I already had my idea for the film, maybe even two. Didn't every movie have at least one sequel?

Write what you know. I'd seldom done that until now, always finding it easier to invent things. Who did I know better than myself, however? And what did I know that could be better than what had happened to me recently?

Let's say there was this female journalist who was assigned to write an article on glamour models, and she became so involved that she stripped off her clothes and posed for a series of nude photographs. Not only that, but then another nude model joined her. They started off by posing together, but then did far more together – and soon they were joined by the photographer. Wouldn't that make a good erotic movie? I knew it would, and I was sure I could write it and make it seem convincing . . .

Perhaps I'd have to make the photographer a man, however. Porn movies seemed to need cocks as well as cunts. One man, two girls, that should work.

Then in the sequel the same intrepid journalist could enter the world of sex films, but unlike myself she would actually take part in the movie in order to add verisimilitude to her report. It could be made as a behind-the-scenes documentary, showing the actors getting ready for their parts. I remembered the girl who had sucked Bob's prick just to give him an erection. Murphy hadn't even thought that worth filming.

I had so many ideas I didn't know where to begin, and I'd filled several pages in my notebook before I got home. Then when I switched on my computer I didn't know where to begin.

At first I tried writing descriptions of locations, making cast lists, until I realised none of that mattered. It was all as superfluous as trying to think of what costumes everyone should wear – because they wouldn't be wearing them for very long.

Then I tried formatting the script the way it should be done, with directions on one line, then dialogue on the next, with each character's name in capitals, but it seemed to take far too long. It slowed down the natural rhythm of my creative flow, and so I gave up.

I did what I knew best: I wrote it as fiction, like a story, and told it all in the first person. Once it was complete, I could play around with my computer keyboard, changing whatever I needed to at the touch of a button.

And so I wrote and wrote and wrote, losing all track of time. Then the phone rang.

"Are you naked?" asked the voice at the other end of the line.

"Don! Where are you? I've been trying to find you. What's happened? Are you alright?"

"I asked you first," he said. "Are you naked?"

I was. It was a hot, sultry night, and what I'd been writing wasn't the kind of thing to keep my temperature down.

"Might be," I said, and I ran my fingertip around my right nipple. "I might be stroking my tits right now."

"What? I can't hear you very well. Did you say you were sick right now?"

"No, no. Why are you phoning? Do you know what time it is?"

"Are you speaking metaphysically or in the existential sense?"

"Are you drunk, Don?"

"I certainly am."

"Where are you?"

"I'm in Hollywood," he said.

"Very funny."

"Hollywood," he said again.

"Hollywood?" I repeated, and I now believed him. This was something Don wouldn't joke about.

"I signed the contract a few hours ago."

"The film deal?" I whispered

"What else?"

"Fan-fucking-tastic! Congratulations! So that's where you've been. Why didn't you tell me?"

"I wanted everything signed and sealed first. Have you got a passport?"

"Passport? Yes. Why?" I'd never been anywhere, but I had a passport just in case.

"Good, because you're flying out to Las Vegas."

"Las Vegas? But—"

"Then we're flying on together to an island in the Caribbean."

"The Caribbean!"

"Is there an echo on this phone?" asked Don. "Las Vegas, then the Caribbean, I know you always wanted to go there. A courier will bring you your tickets tomorrow morning. Are you still there? Say something."

But I said nothing.

"Hello, hello!"

"Are you sure about this, Don?"

"I'm sure. I want you to fly out and meet me."

"Why Las Vegas?"

"So we can get married."

I dropped the phone. When I picked it up the line was dead. The phone rang again half a minute later.

"Married?" I said.

"That's right. I thought it would be a good idea. You agree?"

"Er . . ."

"Does that mean 'yes' or 'no'?"

"You only want to get married so you can get inside my knickers, don't you?"

"Yes. Why else?"

"Er . . ."

"I may be drunk, but I've never been more serious. I'll call you tomorrow morning. Or you can call me. Reverse the charges. I'll give you the number."

I wrote down the number of the hotel where Don was staying.

"How about it?" he asked. "Las Vegas, the Caribbean?"

"Yeah, okay. I've nothing else to do tomorrow."

"Thanks for the enthusiasm. I'll call you again. Goodbye."

"Goodbye."

The line went dead again. I held the receiver in my hand for a while before hanging up. A Caribbean island? It was my dream come true. The only catch was that I'd be there on my honeymoon. I felt like a character in the worst kind of romance novel. Don was hardly the ideal rugged hero, tall and lean and strong and dominant, but he'd suddenly become rich and successful and had proposed to me. Or almost proposed.

If the formula wasn't quite the way it should have been, it was true in one respect. Like every ideal heroine, I was still a virgin.

Somehow I'd never got around to fucking, although I was very good on the theory and had recently attended practical demonstrations.

I went back and sat in front of the computer screen. It was true what I'd told Don; I had nothing else to do to-morrow. What I'd written for Murphy was almost complete. If the ticket arrived, I might as well fly out to Las Vegas. As for getting married, I wasn't too sure about that. Knowing Don, he'd probably be late.

And there was no reason why we couldn't have a Caribbean honeymoon without a wedding.

Angela's photos were spread out on the desk around me. I'd been using them for inspiration while I wrote my own movie script. I picked one up and raised it to the light. It was of me, naked except for a leather jacket and pair of boots. I smiled, imagining it as the author's photo on the jacket of my first book, and I wondered if I ever would get around to writing one.

Suddenly I had an idea. I'd written a film about it, so why not a book? A book about myself and my recent sexual adventures. Write about what you know, I thought, and I smiled at the idea. It was something I could do when I returned from the Caribbean.

The Caribbean . . .

I glanced around my flat, wondering if I would ever return. Would Don come back, or was he planning on staying in Hollywood? If so, would I stay with him?

I shook my head. Everything had happened far too quickly over recent weeks – and it seemed this was only the beginning.

I glanced at the screen, at what I'd been writing when the phone rang. The episode was a version of my adventures with Angela and Dawn. Written in the first-person, "I" was myself, Dawn had become "Patti" and I'd made the photographer a man, but now I realised the name I'd given to the male character.

'Don came closer, his camera aimed at me.

"Wider," he said.

He wasn't talking about my smile, and so I spread my legs even more, slipping my fingers through my pubic hairs and down over the lips of my cunt, holding back my labia as I stroked my swollen clitoris.

"Great, great, great!"

I noticed that he was rapidly losing his professional detachment; his erect cock was clearly outlined within the fabric of his denims. It was that hard male flesh which I needed deep inside me.

But it was Patti who got her hands on Don's pants first,

tugging at the top of his zip with one hand, unbuckling his belt with the other. I joined in immediately, and together we soon had Don's jeans down around his ankles. He offered little resistance, being more concerned to protect his camera. We pulled him onto the bed with us, laughing as we did so, disposing of all his clothes in under a minute. He lay on his back, still holding the camera so it wouldn't get damaged.

Patti reached for the camera, and I used the opportunity to reach for Don's hard tool. It felt hot between my hands, pulsing with virility, and I sensed it grow even more at my touch. I leaned closer, smelling the heady aroma of aroused manhood.

Then I heard a 'click' behind me. Don had become my modelling partner, Patti the photographer.

"Put it in your mouth," she told me.

She didn't need to ask twice; she didn't even need to ask once. I opened my mouth, thrusting out my tongue and gliding its tip along the length of Don's rampant penis.

He sighed in appreciation, stroking my hair, urging me to take him between my lips.

However much I wanted to, I resisted for as long as I could, guiding his knob over my cheeks and my neck, feeling it slide across my smooth flesh, before directing it back towards my mouth and running it across my moist lips. Then my tongue lapped across the purple head, and I let my saliva drip down the shaft as if it were spunk overflowing from my mouth.

"Great, great, great!" said Patti, as she took more photographs.

Don groaned in ecstasy, thrusting his hips forward, silently pleading with me to swallow him down. I teased him even more, at first seeming to obey, opening my mouth wide and breathing onto his throbbing glans, but then drawing my lips away. I leaned further back, and I slid my hand slowly up and down his rigid length. It was slick with my spit.

Don and I looked at each other, and I was about to go down upon him, this time to draw as much of his flesh between my lips as possible. But before I could move, he suddenly grabbed my arms, rolled me over, and a moment later I was on my back. Don lay above me, and I gasped as his knob glided across my twat. He rubbed the domed tip of his phallus over my clit and I moaned with pleasure.

"Wider," he said.

I obeyed, his cock slid deep into my cunt – and we began to fuck.'

There was only one reason to fly out to Las Vegas, which was so that I could finally get myself well and truly fucked. That was what I'd do tomorrow, but first I had to make it through the night.

I'd turned myself on with what my fingers had produced on the keyboard. Now it was time for those same fingers to bring myself off, to satisfy my unfulfilled lust, the burning desire which had been building up deep within for so long and which craved orgasmic release. I licked my fingertips, sliding them down between my thighs and into my wet cunt. And as I started lazily masturbating, I kept on reading and anticipating tomorrow.